Secrets of the Heart

By Pearl S. Buck

FICTION

EAST WIND: WEST WIND, 1930

THE GOOD EARTH, 1931

SONS, 1932

THE FIRST WIFE AND OTHER STORIES, 1933

THE MOTHER, 1934

A HOUSE DIVIDED, 1935

HOUSE OF EARTH [*trilogy of* The Good Earth, *revised,* Sons, *and* A House Divided], 1935

THIS PROUD HEART, 1938

THE PATRIOT, 1939

OTHER GODS, 1941

TODAY AND FOREVER, 1941

DRAGON SEED, 1942

THE PROMISE, 1943

PORTRAIT OF A MARRIAGE, 1945

THE TOWNSMAN [as John Sedges], 1945

PAVILION OF WOMEN, 1946

THE ANGRY WIFE [as John Sedges], 1947

FAR AND NEAR: STORIES OF JAPAN, CHINA, AND AMERICA, 1947

PEONY, 1948

KINFOLK, 1949

THE LONG LOVE [as John Sedges], 1949

GOD'S MEN, 1951

BRIGHT PROCESSION [as John Sedges], 1952

THE HIDDEN FLOWER, 1952

VOICES IN THE HOUSE [as John Sedges], 1953

COME, MY BELOVED, 1953

IMPERIAL WOMAN, 1956

LETTER FROM PEKING, 1957

COMMAND THE MORNING, 1959

FOURTEEN STORIES, 1961

A BRIDGE FOR PASSING, 1962

THE LIVING REED, 1963

DEATH IN THE CASTLE, 1965

THE TIME IS NOON, 1967

THE NEW YEAR, 1968

THE GOOD DEED, 1969

THE THREE DAUGHTERS OF MADAME LIANG, 1969

MANDALA, 1970

THE GODDESS ABIDES, 1972

ALL UNDER HEAVEN, 1973

THE RAINBOW, 1974

EAST AND WEST, 1975

SECRETS OF THE HEART, 1976

TRANSLATION

ALL MEN ARE BROTHERS [SHUI HU CHÜAN], 1933

GENERAL

IS THERE A CASE FOR FOREIGN MISSIONS? [*pamphlet*], 1932

THE EXILE, 1936

FIGHTING ANGEL, 1936

THE CHINESE NOVEL, 1939

OF MEN AND WOMEN, 1941
AMERICAN UNITY AND ASIA, 1942
WHAT AMERICA MEANS TO ME, 1943
THE SPIRIT AND THE FLESH [combining The Exile and Fighting Angel], 1944
TALK ABOUT RUSSIA, with Masha Scott, 1945
TELL THE PEOPLE, 1945
HOW IT HAPPENS: TALK ABOUT THE GERMAN PEOPLE, 1914–1933, with Erna von Pustau, 1947
AMERICAN ARGUMENT, with Eslanda Goode Robeson, 1949
THE CHILD WHO NEVER GREW, 1950
MY SEVERAL WORLDS, 1954
FRIEND TO FRIEND, with Carlos P. Romulo, 1958
THE JOY OF CHILDREN, 1964

CHILDREN FOR ADOPTION, 1965
THE GIFTS THEY BRING, with Gweneth T. Zarfoss, 1965
FOR SPACIOUS SKIES: JOURNEY IN DIALOGUE, with Theodore F. Harris, 1966
TO MY DAUGHTERS, WITH LOVE, 1967
CHINA AS I SEE IT, 1970
THE KENNEDY WOMEN, 1970
THE STORY BIBLE, 1971
CHINA: PAST AND PRESENT, 1972
A COMMUNITY SUCCESS STORY, with Elisabeth Waechter, 1972
ONCE UPON A CHRISTMAS, 1972
PEARL BUCK'S ORIENTAL COOKBOOK, 1972
WORDS OF LOVE, 1974

JUVENILE

THE YOUNG REVOLUTIONIST, 1932
STORIES FOR LITTLE CHILDREN, 1940
THE CHINESE CHILDREN NEXT DOOR, 1942
THE WATER-BUFFALO CHILDREN, 1943
THE DRAGON FISH, 1944
YU LAN: FLYING BOY OF CHINA, 1945
THE BIG WAVE, 1948
ONE BRIGHT DAY, 1950
THE MAN WHO CHANGED CHINA: THE STORY OF SUN YAT-SEN, 1953
JOHNNY JACK AND HIS BEGINNINGS, 1954

THE BEECH TREE, 1955
CHRISTMAS MINIATURE, 1957
MY SEVERAL WORLDS [Abridged for Younger Readers], 1957
THE CHRISTMAS GHOST, 1960
WELCOME CHILD, 1964
THE BIG FIGHT, 1965
THE LITTLE FOX IN THE MIDDLE, 1966
MATTHEW, MARK, LUKE AND JOHN, 1967
THE CHINESE STORY TELLER, 1971
A GIFT FOR THE CHILDREN, 1973
MRS. STARLING'S PROBLEM, 1973

Secrets of the Heart

STORIES BY

Pearl S. Buck

The John Day Company NEW YORK

Designed by Ingrid Beckman
Manufactured in the United States of America

Library of Congress Cataloging in Publication Data

Buck, Pearl Sydenstricker, 1892–1973.
    Secrets of the heart.

        CONTENTS: Wonderful woman.—Here and now.—Morning in the park. [etc.]
        I. Title.
PZ3.B8555Se5 [PS3503.U198]   813'.5'2   76-6550
ISBN 0-381-98287-4

10 9 8 7 6 5 4 3 2 1

Contents

Wonderful Woman

Elinor Brame lingered a moment at the cemetery gate. There was a great crowd, for of course everyone had come to Mrs. Seabury's funeral. There were delegates from all the organizations in town, even the fire department. There were rich people and poor—Mrs. Crotherton was there, very handsome in her dark furs, but so was old Mollie Daley there—very properly, because Mrs. Seabury had kept her on as laundress for years when everyone knew how bad she was at laundering. But as Mrs. Seabury herself said, "I often tell Mollie she does nothing well, but she does less damage in the laundry than elsewhere. The only time I let her come upstairs she broke my hawthorne vase. It was a wedding present."

Mollie had sobbed heartily beside the open grave, though she must have known Grant Seabury would keep her on. "I want everything exactly as Mother had it," he told Elinor in a low, intense voice. As soon as she heard that Mrs. Seabury had died she had gone over to see what she could do. "Nothing is to be changed," he had said, looking about the pleasant, conventional living room. "Father and I both feel so. Besides, everything Mother did was perfect."

It had been almost as though Mrs. Seabury had

directed her own funeral. Everyone whispered to everyone else, "This is just what she would have wanted, isn't it?" They all behaved as though she were not dead. Indeed, it seemed as though Mrs. Seabury's voice must come rushing out of heaven, fresh and strong and kind, "It's been a *beautiful* funeral—exactly what I wanted. Thank you all so much!"

"Ashes unto ashes—dust unto dust," the rector of St. Grace's had chanted. But no one dreamed he was speaking of Mrs. Seabury. Elinor saw Grant's handsome face lift proudly to the sky. A little snow was falling but he seemed not to notice. Mr. Seabury did not look up. He had stared steadily down into the grave and he kept staring down there.

People now were gathering around the two tall men, impulsively and warmly. They looked very much alike for the moment, Grant and his father, although Mrs. Seabury had always said gaily that Grant was *her* son. They stood side by side. Grant was saying quickly, "Thank you—thank you very much—my mother would have appreciated—" but Mr. Seabury merely muttered, "Yes—yes—yes—"

"Come, Father," she heard Grant say decisively, "we must go home—it's getting very cold." He took his father's arm, and people parted to let them pass down the walk to the gate.

Elinor had slipped away as soon as the organ began to play the final strains of "For all the saints who from their labors rest." She was very cold and she wanted to go home. She had left her small green runabout conveniently near the gate. No one could have made her come to a funeral except Mrs. Seabury. But Mrs. Seabury would have said in her straightforward clear way, "Of course you will come, Elinor. I should be very hurt if you didn't—and so would Grant."

So she came.

Funerals! When she was ready to die she was going to slip away somewhere and throw herself into a volcano or into the sea, where there'd be nothing left to bury. And then at the gate she looked back and caught sight of Grant's face. It was the terrified face of a small, lonely boy. It was only a moment. When she looked again it was Grant's face, handsome and very sure.

But because of that moment she waited for him at the gate instead of going on home. They were moving down the path. He was quite near her now, but he did not see her. He was looking down at the path, frowning a little.

"Grant," she said quietly. He looked up.

"Elinor!" he said.

"I'd like to come over for a little while this evening," she said, "if I may."

"Will you?" he asked eagerly. "We'll be very glad—won't we, Father?"

"Yes," Mr. Seabury murmured, "yes, of course—" He did not look up. With his stick he pushed a bit of mud from his slim, polished black shoe.

"Why not drive back with us now?" Grant pressed her.

"I have my car here," she replied. "Besides, if you don't mind, I'd rather come later." She nodded at the crowds and instantly Grant understood. Of course it would be better if she did not go back with them directly. It was not as if she were anything more than a friend.

"It's awfully good of you," he said.

She smiled without reply and turned to her car.

She was driving along the oak-lined street which ended in the big house. It was impossible to imagine the house without Mrs. Seabury. People said, laughing a little, that it had been like Mrs. Seabury to set her house so that the finest street in town led up to it as though it were a private driveway. But at the same time they were proud of the solid, columned square of red brick. If they were driving strangers they nodded carelessly at it and said, "That's Mrs. Seabury's house. Know her? She is the only woman ever ran for mayor in our town—nearly got it, too—wonderful woman she is."

Elinor drove her car swiftly down the street. Ahead of her in the two strong beams of light she could see the oak leaves whirling in the wind above the concrete, flickering in and out of the light. She drove through them and around into the circle before the house. Tonight at dinner, alone with her father, since her mother was dead, he had said, "I wish you'd take James and my car, Elinor, at night." But she had replied briskly, "I shan't be late, thanks, Father. I'll just drop in to see how Grant is—the first evening—"

"Yes," said Mr. Brame gently. "The first evening is hard." He fell silent and they both remembered the evening after her gay little mother was gone.

"I wish you'd marry again, Father," Elinor said suddenly.

He looked up, startled. "You're young and handsome," she said, smiling. But he did not smile.

"Oh, no," he said, "I couldn't—not after—" He had gone on then in his delicate, precise fashion to say, "I hope, Elinor, that you will not allow the thought of my loneliness to—to delay any plans of your own. I am quite content, you know—as content as I can now be."

"Oh, no," she had said quickly. "I haven't any plans, Father. There isn't anyone I want to marry."

She brought her car to a standstill. She liked driving

her own car. And she could not bear the thought of James, waiting outside in the darkness. She liked to be free.

Now she went up the steps slowly, drawing off her gloves. The air was damp and cold and she thought for a second of Mrs. Seabury out in the cemetery. Then she rang the bell. She couldn't be sure Mrs. Seabury really was there until she had gone into this house.

The door opened, and the butler smiled at her as he had when she was a little girl. "Good evening, Miss Elinor," he said, "Mr. Grant—"

But Grant was already there, his head looming above Rhodes's white head.

"Get out of my way, Rhodes, there's a good chap," he was saying. "I'll see to things. Come in, Elinor. I've been waiting."

She went in and he took her coat and hat eagerly. For a moment she did not speak. It seemed impossible to believe that a pleasantly sharp voice would not call from the library, "Is that you, dear Elinor? Come in—I'm here!"

She waited, listening.

"Doesn't it seem as if she would speak at any moment?" Grant asked breathlessly. "I keep waiting—"

"Yes, I know," she replied. She put out her hand for a quick second and touched his.

"Dad's there, of course," said Grant. He took her elbow and led her to the library.

Everything was exactly as it had always been. The wood fire burned and before it on a table was a coffee tray. Mr. Seabury sat in his chair, his hands on his knees, waiting.

"We were just going to have our coffee," he said in his high voice. "Will you have some, Elinor?"

"Indeed I will," she said, smiling at him. "How lovely the fire is!"

She sat down and Grant picked up a log and threw it on the fire.

"Yes," said Mr. Seabury vaguely. His look was worried. "Grant?" he whispered. Up the chimney the sparks flew and the wood crackled. He turned.

"Yes, Dad?" Grant asked.

"Who'll pour the coffee?"

The chair in which Mrs. Seabury always sat was now in the corner by the door. Rhodes perhaps had put it there to make it unobtrusive.

"Elinor?" Grant turned to her and changed his look. "No," he said abruptly, "I will do it myself—in a minute." He arranged the log carefully. No one spoke. Then he turned and stooped over the low table and poured the coffee. His hand, touching the silver pot, trembled a little. But he began to speak in his eager fashion.

"Was it raining when you came in, Elinor? I hope it isn't going to rain—not at once—November rain is so impossible."

He handed a cup to her and another to his father as he talked.

"No," she said quietly, "it's not raining. There is a feel of more snow, rather. There are no stars."

Mr. Seabury was stirring his coffee slowly.

"I remember," he began vaguely, "that the year your mother and I were married, Grant—thirty-one years ago that was—yesterday—the snow fell so early and the train was delayed because of drifts, and we couldn't get away as soon as we had planned."

"Mother died on her wedding anniversary," Grant said. He looked at Elinor and she saw his eyes shining with tears.

"Yes," said Mr. Seabury. He lifted his cup and drank the coffee at a gulp and suddenly he stood up. "I think I'll go upstairs," he said. He hesitated a moment. "No," he murmured half to himself, "I won't say goodnight. Maybe I'll be back—"

He walked softly out of the room, avoiding Mrs. Seabury's chair. The room was very quiet.

"Well, Grant?" she said, leaning back and looking at him. He would want to talk and talk—had she not known him all her life? She would open the gate for him.

"Elinor!" he said. "I am so glad you came tonight!"

He sat down in his father's chair and she studied him. He had on the dark suit he had worn all day, and above it his long, handsome head rose with great dignity. He was very handsome—a shade too dignified perhaps to be not yet twenty-seven. But even as a little boy he had held himself aloof from them all. Other boys had not quite called him a sissy because he did everything so well. He rode well, for his mother had given him a pony when he was eight, and he was generous about letting other children ride it. He bent himself to baseball with terrible intensity and played it well, though he never became the captain of the team. But Mrs. Seabury had sent him away to Andover rather early and then most of the other boys, going to public school at home, forgot him. When he came home for vacations he danced so well they were all inclined to think after all he was a sissy, except that he was so generous with the small car his mother gave him when he was eighteen. Half the time he walked because he had lent it to some other boy. When Bobbie Lee wrecked it at last and came to tell him, miserable and contrite, Grant had been fabulously generous.

"It doesn't matter," he kept saying, "it's all right,

Bob—don't feel bad. I don't use it much at school any-way."

"Oh gosh," Bobbie groaned, "if there was any way I could pay it back."

"It might have happened anyway to me, sometime—it was an accident, wasn't it?" Grant said. In a moment he was cheerfully talking of something else.

After that Bobbie raged at anyone who said sissy about Grant Seabury. Besides, Grant won Phi Beta Kappa and played football, too, at college. There was simply nothing to say to a man like that. And after college he had stayed on with a fellowship, partly studying literature, partly teaching.

"Grant wants to write," his mother said. Elinor could remember Mrs. Seabury's strong, capable white hands as they manipulated these very coffee cups one Sunday evening.

"He's getting good experience where he is."

Mr. Seabury had been sitting then where Grant was sitting now. He had begun saying something in his murmuring voice about life being the best preparation. But Mrs. Seabury had cut in rather sharply.

"Well, Grant's living, isn't he? If you mean running around doing wild things—personally, I've never thought that was life."

Mr. Seabury had not answered, and in a little while he excused himself and went upstairs. Now that she thought of it, indeed, he was nearly always excusing himself and going upstairs. Evening after evening she and Mrs. Seabury had sat here alone, and she was willing to sit, because soon Mrs. Seabury would begin to talk about Grant. She came time after time to this quiet house to hear this talk about Grant. Mrs. Seabury, not long before the attack of pneumonia of which she died, had said one night as Elinor rose to go home, "It is such a pleasure to talk to someone who understands Grant."

She had touched Elinor's arm in her undemonstrative fashion.

"I've always been very fond of Grant," Elinor said quietly.

"And he of you," Mrs. Seabury said warmly. "He always wants you to come to dinner his second night home. The first night he keeps for me."

Yes, Elinor knew that. She had for years kept those second nights of Grant's vacations free, waiting for Mrs. Seabury's voice over the telephone to say, "Elinor dear, Grant comes home day after tomorrow. Will you come to us the evening after?—Not a party, you know—"

"Thank you, Mrs. Seabury," Elinor always replied, "I'd love to come." Once she nearly sang back, "It's always a party for us when Grant comes home." That was the summer after his graduation, when he had gone straight to Europe and had not come home until October. But she knew Mrs. Seabury would not have liked it and so she said only what she always said. She knew why Mrs. Seabury kept asking her. Mrs. Seabury had said more than once, "I can trust Grant with you, Elinor. Girls are so dreadful nowadays. They tempt young men so. I know you are above that."

She looked at Grant now. He was listening to something, frowning a little.

"I do believe Father—" he was saying.

They both listened. From upstairs a faint piping music floated down.

"He's playing his flute!" Grant exclaimed. "It's the most amazing thing—I can't understand him."

"You mean?" she inquired. The melody faltered, slipped off key, then righted itself again, and she recognized it as "Annie Laurie."

"How he can—amuse himself—tonight," Grant said, "when he knows how Mother hated his flute!"

"Did she?" Elinor asked. "Why?"

"Oh, it's such a futile, silly thing," he said. He poured himself another cup of coffee, forgetting her. "I don't mind telling you, Elinor, I don't think my father was good enough for her."

"I suppose a good many people felt that," she said gently. "It's funny," she added, "I never heard him play the flute. I never knew he did."

"He's played for years," Grant said, "although he has no ear. Mother's ear was very keen. It was agony to her when she came in at night, tired with the really important things she did, to have to hear that stringy wailing. But all she asked was that he go up to the attic to play. Evening after evening he's left her here alone, when I wasn't here, and gone up there." Grant broke off to listen. "He's in his own room tonight, though," he added. "I'm sorry—it's painful, isn't it?" He winced as the melody rose, dragging, slipping a little.

"I don't mind it," she said, smiling over the edge of her coffee cup. "I haven't a very good ear."

He put down his cup and went to the window and drew aside the curtain and stared out.

"It is snowing," he said suddenly.

"It's better than rain," she answered.

He turned. "Yes—how do you know how I feel?"

"I know," she said quietly. "My own mother died."

"I forgot." He came over to her impulsively. Then suddenly he bent and took up her hand and kissed it. She was so surprised she began to tremble. He had never touched her before—not once—beyond the warm, swift handshake which she could never be sure was warmer than he gave to anyone else.

"Grant is *clean*," Mrs. Seabury had said once when they were sitting alone. "I never worry." She had not answered and Mrs. Seabury had withdrawn quickly from this side of Grant. Now she felt his lips, hot and hard upon the palm of her hand. He put her hand down quickly, without speaking, and began to stir the fire in his energetic fashion. She closed her hand and held his kiss. Her heart was beating so hard she felt a little dizzy. The flames burst out of the glowing logs.

"I suppose," he said abruptly, "it's that she was more to me than just a mother—she *is* more to me. She was so wonderful—as a woman—a person—"

She did not answer. In her palm the kiss was burning like a coal, like a jewel, like the fragment of a star.

He was sitting before the fire, his hands clasped about his knees.

"You know," he said thoughtfully, "Mother could have been the mayor that time she ran for office, but she gave it up."

His head was so near her knee that she could have put out her hand and drawn it there. She did not move. He turned his dark eyes upon her. "Do you know why?"

"Tell me," she said. It was the sound of his voice that mattered.

"She found that it was impossible to run this town without having to listen to that gang in Third Street. They had their men in every important place in the city. And she wouldn't be run by them. She decided that she would rather be free to go into what they were doing and break up their power. She did, too. Those articles of hers the newspapers ran finished the gang. She got the people so worked up the police had to go after Jim Connally and his bunch. They moved to New York." He paused. "We used to beg her not to sit downstairs in the evening with the shades all up. She might have been killed. But you couldn't scare her. She said, 'If they kill me, everybody will know what I've been saying is true.'" His voice trembled. He got up suddenly and stood before her, and thrust his hands into his pockets. He was staring at her, but she knew he did not see her. "No one really knew her except me," he said. "I wish to God that I could make everyone see what she was." His voice grew passionate. "When I think that it's over—her life—her being—when I think that all she was—lies out there—finished—buried—I could—shoot myself!" He leaned on the mantelpiece and put his head on his arms.

She was terrified. She leaped up and put her arm over his shoulders.

"Oh, no," she cried. "Grant, how she'd scold you if she heard you! I'm surprised at you!"

He was listening to her. His body was tense with listening. She hurried on. "Why, it would be so ungrateful of you—if you go on living and working, she isn't all dead. You are a part of her—she felt that so much."

"I feel there's nothing I can really do without her." His voice came despondent and muffled.

"All those books she expected you to write," she reminded him. She had drawn her arm quickly away when he did not move. He moved now, not toward her, but to walk about impatiently.

"I haven't anything to say," he cried. "I can't think of anything else—except her. She was very young, you know, Elinor—only forty-nine. Why, we thought our life was ahead of us—hers and mine. My father isn't interested in the same things. I can't think of other people—imagine novels about them, I mean. No, I think I'll persuade Dad to travel with me—I have to look after him and I might as well—Egypt, perhaps! and India— she always wanted to go to India and we'd planned to go when she had time."

She stood, thinking quickly. How could she keep him from going away—from leaving her?

"Why don't you write about her, then?" she asked.

"*Write* about her?" he repeated.

"Yes," she said, "biography, if you like—or maybe a novel, making people see her as you did. It would make her live on."

"Yes," he said, slowly. "It would, wouldn't it!"

They looked at each other intensely. He was not thinking about her, but she was thinking only of him, feeling him, denying herself, giving to him not herself but this other woman who was his mother.

"I believe I could do it." He was walking about the room. "I believe—would a novel or a biography be better, Elinor? Biography—though of course she was only beginning to be nationally known through those lectures she started three years ago for women. She came to see that one reason why woman suffrage hasn't accomplished more is because women are not accustomed to thinking about politics and don't know how to begin. They were very popular—her lectures. She put things so clearly, always." He was planning as he walked. "Yes, I believe a biography, full of stories about her, you know, but all true. That's what I'd like." He stopped beside her. "Elinor, my dear, you've given me something. You've given me my mother back again."

She did not answer. They stood looking at each other. From upstairs came the thin wailing of Mr. Seabury's flute. He was playing, very slowly and mournfully,

"Scots wha hae wi' Wallace bled." Grant turned away impatiently.

"That noise—"

But she stopped him. "Don't," she said. "How do you know what comforts him? People get comfort in such queer ways." She hurried on. "Sit down—let's think about the book."

He sat down and forgot the flute.

"Yes," he said eagerly, "it can be a very important thing. I begin to see that. In fact, it can hardly fail to be."

The flute had stopped. Mr. Seabury was coming downstairs quietly. The door opened and there he was. He looked refreshed, almost as though he had been asleep.

"Well, well!" he said.

"We've thought of something, Father!" Grant said eagerly.

"You have?" Mr. Seabury inquired mildly.

"A biography—about Mother!"

Mr. Seabury sat down and put his hands on his knees and considered seriously.

"That would be a fine thing to do," he said, "a mighty fine thing. She's the sort of person that would be fine in a book."

He paused and stared into the fire.

"I wish I knew more about her childhood," Grant said passionately. "I wish I knew everything about her!"

Mr. Seabury did not answer.

"When did you first know her, Mr. Seabury?" Elinor asked gently.

Mr. Seabury started slightly and looked up. His eyes were a limpid blue and his gray hair was as curly as a baby's. There was something infantile, indeed, about his simple, rosy face.

"Ethel?" he asked. "Oh, I guess I always knew Ethel. Her family moved here from the West when she was a baby, and before I was born. She was just a little older than I was—just enough to give her the advantage over me, you might say. They lived right next door to us. She used to say she brought me up—guess she did, too, in a way."

"What was she like when she was a young girl?" Grant asked eagerly.

"No," Elinor interrupted. "Let's begin at the beginning. What's your first memory of her, Mr. Seabury?"

Mr. Seabury considered, his face wrinkling. He was staring into the fire again.

"Well," he said unwillingly, "she was always strong for her age, Ethel was. She used to push the other children around quite a bit." He chuckled. "Once she came sailing out of Sunday school in one of those big straw hats with streamers and her skirts stiff and starched and she says to me, 'I'm not going to fight any more, George Seabury,' she says. 'Teacher says it's wicked. And if anybody wants to fight me, I'll knock him down.' " He laughed. "Don't know why I remember that, but I do."

They all laughed, and Elinor asked, "Is that the first time you remember her?"

"No," said Mr. Seabury, "no, I don't know that it is. Fact is, I can't remember any first time. The earliest I can remember, Ethel was already there. It seems she was always there."

"Just as now," Grant said in a low voice, "it doesn't seem possible she isn't here."

They fell into silence and Elinor sat, delicately feeling the differing mournfulness of the two men. She seemed herself not to exist at all. There were only Mrs. Seabury and these two men whose lives she had made.

"She was wonderful," she murmured wistfully. Yes, she must have been wonderful to have held Grant's love so strongly through childhood and youth, until now.

"She was more than that," Grant said. "She was everything a human being could be. She had a man's mind and reason, and a woman's heart. There'll never be anybody like her."

Elinor got up abruptly.

"I must be going home," she said. "It's late."

"I'll go with you," Grant said and rose.

"No, please," she said. "I'd rather not. I have my car."

"Then I'll get your things, at least," Grant said. He went out and came back again and stood holding her coat. She slipped into it and felt for a moment his touch on her shoulder, his breath on her cheek. For a moment his eyes were near, kind and full of warmth.

"I appreciate so much your thinking of the book," he said. "I can't tell you how different it makes everything—it gives me something to do for her. Here—let me button your coat."

She stood, tense for a moment, while expertly he buttoned the coat.

"I'm used to doing that for Mother," he said. "Now I'll see you into your car."

"Don't bother," she said.

"It's no bother," he replied. "Wait—I'll get an umbrella for the snow." He hurried out and she stood a moment.

"Goodnight, Mr. Seabury," she said.

"Goodnight, my dear," he said. "Thank you for coming. It's made us both less lonely."

She hesitated. "I love your flute," she said in a low voice. Grant would be at the door at any second.

Mr. Seabury looked up with pleasure.

"Do you?" he exclaimed. "Now most people don't appreciate the flute."

"I do," she said. "I hope you keep on at it."

"I intend to," said Mr. Seabury.

"Ready?" Grant was at the door.

"Yes," she said.

They went out. It was snowing very hard and it had turned very cold. They ran through the snow and she found her engine already running. He had come out and started it and turned on the heater. "How nice of you," she said, creeping into the seat. He was shielding her with the umbrella. She had a glimpse of his absorbed, anxious face.

"I hate to let you go alone," he said. "Telephone me when you reach home. The streets will be slippery."

"Yes, I will," she said. She waited a moment. He was so dear. She wanted him to have what he wanted.

"Elinor," he said suddenly, "will you do something for me?"

"Yes," she said, "I will do anything for you, Grant."

"Then help me—to make her book!"

She smiled at him a little sadly.

"Yes," she said again.

"And begin tomorrow?"

She nodded.

"Anything," she said. When she had rounded the circle he was still there in the snow. She waved to him and he waved back to her and she went on.

Mrs. Seabury was not dead, after all. Tomorrow, and day after day, she and Grant were going to resurrect her and bring her back to life. She wished that she had never thought of the book. No, but if she had not, he would have escaped her. He would have gone away and she would have been too proud to pursue him. She drove on into the white lines of snow. They converged like darts of ice flung at her as she passed.

It was as though she and Grant were molding Mrs. Seabury out of clay. They were adding each day to the figure, defining it, rounding it, carving the lines to the looks which made her into the entirety they both knew.

"Let's go back to the very first moment of her life," Grant said the first morning in the library. "I wish my grandparents were living. Now that she's gone, I realize Mother was a very solitary person. No one knew much about her, really."

It was ten o'clock. An hour ago Mr. Seabury had put on his gray overcoat and hat and gone off to work as usual. He was a clerk in the bank of which Elinor's father was president. She could remember the Sunday morning Mrs. Seabury had come to see her father about it. It was just after Mr. Seabury had gone bankrupt for the second time in his shoe business. Elinor had got up to leave the room when Mrs. Seabury came in, but Mrs. Seabury stopped her.

"Don't go, dear child," she had said. "I have no secrets. I've come begging. Mr. Brame, I can't let Harry open the store again. Besides, I haven't—I can't afford— to do it. I've used up nearly a third of my little inheritance on it already and I have to think of Grant." She had looked handsome and quiet and a little pathetic. "I think Harry ought to be under someone else. He simply isn't made to manage for himself."

That was twelve years ago. Mr. Seabury had been going regularly to the bank ever since. Whether he liked the job or not no one knew. No one had ever asked him.

"I suppose we ought to give her family background," Grant was saying. "After all, women like Mother aren't accidents. Her father was a well-known judge—I can just remember him—a tall, dark, white-haired man on a horse."

"Weren't there other children?" she asked. Grant must look like his grandfather. A judge! Yes, and Grant would make a good judge.

"There is a younger brother—a worthless fellow," Grant said. His lips curved downward. "I've never called him uncle. He comes sometimes—my mother always gave him money. She never said much even to me about it. She was so loyal." He paused and went on. "Once when I was a little boy about ten I told a lie. I'll never forget her face. She didn't scold me. She whispered, 'You aren't going to disappoint me, too, are you, Grant?' She was quite pale and she looked so frightened I began to cry." He got up from his chair and walked up and down once and sat down again. "I made up my mind that day I'd be the sort of man she wanted me to be."

"And you are," she said, smiling a little wistfully. There must really have been something wonderful in Mrs. Seabury.

"I try to be," he said. "Well! Let's put down all we know in notes that we can make into an outline." She took up her pencil and he began quickly. "Ancestry, Scotch on her father's side, English on her mother's. Family came to this country in 1753. The first one was a younger, landless son of a baronet and he bought land, but he couldn't farm and he sold again and took up trade with the Orient and grew rich. His two sons went to Harvard. One was a historian later and the younger one was a judge. There's been a judge in almost every generation. My great-grandfather ran for governor of the state and lost it by a narrow vote."

She was taking down the notes rapidly.

"It's so odd," he said restlessly, "I keep forgetting. I've nearly said half a dozen times this morning, 'I'll ask Mother about that.' She's told me all these things, but—"

"Did she leave a diary or anything?" Elinor asked.

He looked at her. "I hadn't thought of that," he exclaimed. "Let's go and look."

They went upstairs together to Mrs. Seabury's door. The last time she had been there was when Mrs. Seabury was lying on the bed under the sheet, dead.

"I told Rhodes nothing was to be touched," Grant said, "but I haven't been here—since."

She touched his hand quickly and he held her hand a moment and let it go. "I'm glad you're here," he said.

He opened the door. The room was very neat, and the yellow satin cover stretched smoothly over the big bed. The shades were drawn halfway, and the sun fell brightly in squares upon the taupe carpet. It was a handsome room, but austere and very silent. It might have been a room in a good hotel except that on the west wall were dozens of pictures of Grant, Grant at all ages.

"Oh, Grant!" Elinor cried, "I've always wanted to look at those pictures!" She forgot Mrs. Seabury and went to them. She had always wanted to look at them closely but she had never been in the room alone and Grant would not notice as Mrs. Seabury would how she looked at them. She gazed intently at his chubby, baby face. It was a grave, steady little face, but the eyes were eager. And the little boy and the bigger boy were the same Grant, conscientious and eager together. He smiled a little shyly now.

"Mother made me have a picture on every birthday," he said. "I used to hate it, but I never told her so. I'm glad I didn't."

But he was not interested in himself. He went to the

mahogany desk in the corner of the room and began to open the drawers. Then he hesitated. "I have never touched this desk before," he said. "I have the oddest feeling about it now—as if it weren't right—"

"Shall I do it?" she asked.

"Do you mind?" he replied.

She did not answer, not knowing whether she minded. She did, for a moment, but perhaps not as much as he did. So she went on while he watched. Everything was very neatly arranged in the drawers. Papers were clasped about with elastics and labeled.

"They're all personal," he said. "Her business correspondence is in her office downtown."

There were a few letters labeled "Harry." They'd been apart so little there hadn't been need for letters. But the big lower drawer was stacked with Grant's letters. "My Son," the label read, neatly typed.

"We won't use those," Grant said quickly.

Yet there were very few letters besides those—almost no letters from friends. In a pigeonhole were three recent letters not held together by anything. Grant opened them, glanced at them, and threw them in the wastebasket.

"Peter—my uncle," he said briefly, "wanting money." He picked one up again and showed her a note at the end of the page in Mrs. Seabury's firm, clear handwriting. "Sent $65.00. All I can afford now and said so." She caught a glimpse of uneven, nervous writing above. "Darling Ethel, I don't know what I would do without such a sister. I promise—"

"I'd never even heard of your uncle," she said. "It's strange."

"You won't think it so if you ever see him," Grant said.

It was at that moment that they found the diary. It was in the deep top drawer of the old-fashioned desk, a big, hard-backed book. Elinor saw it and drew it out.

"Grant, what's this?" she cried.

He leaned over her and opened it. On the first page Mrs. Seabury had written *My Diary*. At the bottom in recent ink she had written, "Note: This diary may be used as a source for any biography of me."

"She thought of everything," Grant said.

"Didn't she!" Elinor agreed. Why did she feel a slight repulsion toward Mrs. Seabury? She turned the page. Mrs. Seabury had begun the book plainly. "In the year 1753—" The writing flowed on, fine and compact, for hundreds of pages. Years ago Mrs. Seabury had practically begun her own biography.

They read it aloud together in the library, taking turns. It was the story of a strong, hardworking woman with a conscience. Even as a little girl she was talking of duty. She had listened to her father when he talked of his cases.

"My father never took his responsibilities lightly," she wrote. "At night when we gathered about the dining table he would tell us of the people upon whose lives he had decided that day. He knew that upon his decision rested human fate. He believed that lack of knowledge was what made criminals. One day a woman was brought in for the murder of her child—her eighth. When asked why she had killed this babe, he said she seemed dazed and muttered that she could not bear to hear it cry any more. My mother was shocked, but my father said when he saw the woman's face he could understand it—she was ignorant and very tired and so poor. As he told the story the resolution of my life began to form. I would devote myself to the enlightenment of women."

The earnest child grew into the earnest girl at college. "I was chosen for the position of president in my class and as such I tried to do more than others before me. The girls were woefully ignorant of life and of their place in the world. I used to give ten minutes at each meeting trying to make them feel their importance as human beings. But most of them had no ambition beyond marriage."

It was the picture of a creature at once austere and pitiful. She had a heart. She ached because others suffered. But she was sternly sure of herself. Then this tall, rigid girl, scornful of marriage, came home from college and within a year was married to Harry Seabury . . .

The factory whistles were blowing. It was noon. They looked up from the closely written pages.

"I must go home," Elinor exclaimed, "but I can scarcely bear to stop. Grant, does your mother seem a little pathetic to you?"

"No," he said. "No—only magnificent!"

The look on his face was reverent. He closed the book and put it on the table. "I won't read until you come back."

"I'll cancel my bridge club," she said. "It's nothing. I'll be back about three, shall I?"

"Thank you," he said.

His look fell upon her and lingered, but she knew he did not see her. He was seeing only that tall, austere girl.

In the afternoon as she drove up the circle, she saw Mr. Seabury. He was sitting on a bench set in a little circle of pines, doing nothing in the sunshine, because it was a Saturday afternoon and the bank was closed. The day had turned suddenly warm, and the brief snow was already gone.

"Good afternoon, Mr. Seabury," she called.

"Hello, Elinor," he called back, and lifted his hand a little toward her. He looked warm and comfortable and half asleep. She thought of the strong, humorless young girl who had married him and felt an intense curiosity to know what he had thought of her. She went over to him.

"Have you time to talk a few minutes?" she asked, sitting down. The pines hid them from the house.

"I haven't anything but time just now," he replied, his voice amiable. "What is it, Elinor?"

"You know Grant and I have begun that biography," she said.

He nodded, and the warm, careless look on his face changed. It grew grave and a little cautious.

"We found a diary," Elinor went on, "but she doesn't tell everything. Will you—would you mind—if sometimes I asked you for your side of the picture?"

"No," he said. "I'll be glad to help." He hesitated. "Ethel and I—we didn't always look at everything the same anyway."

"That's valuable in itself," she said.

"Is there anything you want to know now?" he inquired.

"Yes, there is," she replied. "I want to know how you came to marry each other."

The sunshine of the quiet day poured about them. He did not speak for a moment. With his stick he began pushing together a little heap of brown oak leaves, still wet with the melting snow.

"If you'd rather not—" Elinor said gently.

"It's not that," he said. "I was just trying to remember. I don't know just how it did come about." He retrieved a leaf and pushed it with the others. "I didn't want to finish college. I had some notion I didn't want to go on with my dad's shoe business and I did want to go on the stage. Why the stage? I don't know, except I'd been in a college play or two. I did comic stuff and people laughed." He paused a moment, then went on again. "She'd finished college that June and she was at home sort of waiting to see what she was going to do. She was talking some of studying law and taking up after her father. I came home one summer—sophomore year it was—not wanting to go back to college. And we'd always been friends, in a way, though I'd never gone out with her much. She wasn't the sort of girl you'd take to a dance exactly, though she danced well enough. But somehow the fellows just didn't. Well, I told her I didn't want to go back to college. And she thought I was wrong. She felt it was her duty to make me see I ought to get a good education. I was honestly on the fence about it, and I went over a good deal to see her. I respected her opinion—I always did respect Ethel's opinion." A passing wind scattered the leaves and he began pushing them together again. "She was a fine-looking girl—tall, and her hair was straight and fair and her eyebrows were level across her eyes—gray eyes, you know. She was honest, too, and just. She threw herself into helping me decide what I ought to do. I couldn't keep from admiring her for her fairness—she always tried to see both sides. One evening"—he cleared his throat—"it was just before I was to go back to college—if I was going—I was at her home. We were sitting side by side on an old couch they had—and I just suddenly saw that Ethel was a grand girl—the sort of girl you could give yourself to and know that she'd never let you down—she had integrity—that was Ethel. And I said, 'Why do you care what I do, Ethel?' And she looked surprised and as though she'd been caught. She thought a second and answered as honestly as could be, 'I don't know—but I do care, terribly.' And something—I don't know what—made me lean over and take her in my arms. I'd never touched her before. She wasn't that kind of a girl. I'd never thought of it. But if I had—I'd have imagined she was sort of stiff—and hard." He stopped a moment. "She wasn't, though," he went on in a lower voice. "She was soft as anything—and warm. She sort of—clung to me—that day—and I kissed her." He looked up abruptly. "That's all, I guess. When I came into that house I hadn't an idea I'd go out of it engaged to her. But I did. There wasn't any more talk about college or stage. I went straight into the business and we got married."

"Did your parents approve?" Elinor asked.

"Everybody respected Ethel," he replied. He chuckled. "I remember my dad said, 'If anybody can make anything of you, she can.' "

A shadow fell across his face. "She tried, I suppose," he said. "I don't know—it's funny—but I really wanted to do what Ethel wanted me to do—but I just didn't, somehow. I mean—I knew she was right. She was always right. But somehow she just—made you not want to do it. I'm of a contrary disposition, maybe. Grant never has been that way." He stirred restlessly. "The funniest thing is that now she isn't here—I want to do what she wanted me to. Saturday afternoon I've always bowled. Well, she didn't like the crowd down there at Hiley's—but I always went anyway. But here I am, sitting on a bench, Saturday afternoon—"

Elinor laughed and got up. Grant would be in the library, impatient to begin.

"I hope she knows it," she said.

Mr. Seabury shook his head. "I don't even enjoy my flute as much as I did," he said mournfully. "But I'm going to keep on with it, just the same."

By the library fire Grant was reading aloud to her again.

"My long friendship with Harry Seabury now changed quickly into something more. I say quickly, and yet I know that I had always felt a sense of protection over him. He was an impulsive, eager boy who was often in trouble, both as a child and a youth. He was not a student, and even in the public high school, which we attended together, I felt a responsibility for him, so that I helped him prepare for examinations, especially in mathematics in which I excelled and he found difficult. I had little time for boys, however, after I went to college, although Harry and I, being neighbors, saw each other at vacations. It was after I had been graduated that I found my childhood friendship crystallizing into something more. It happened that he wished not to return to college and I tried to persuade him it was his duty to finish. I believe in education. But during the holidays we found we cared for each other and the matter was decided. We were married in five months. I entered into this relationship with the most solemn devotion, vowing to myself that never, in the slightest most secret way would I deviate from my loyalty to my husband. To the best of my knowledge I never have."

Grant looked up.

"She never did," he said. His eyes were shining and his mouth was tender. "She lifted marriage up. I remember once that a woman—you know, Mrs. Cassels— came to see Mother. It was when she was beginning to be so unhappy and there was talk of her divorcing Cassels. I remember hearing someone crying here in this very room. I wanted to ask Mother something and I opened the door a little and I heard her say—you know how strong and kind her voice was—'It doesn't matter what he does, dear Mrs. Cassels, it's you. It's your duty to *make* your marriage right, by endurance, by patient suffering, if necessary, glorifying it alone, if he will not help you.' I shut the door and went away. And Mrs. Cassels went back to her husband."

"She ran away with someone else, later, didn't she?" Elinor asked. She remembered pretty Mrs. Cassels and her husband who took drugs.

"That was several years after," Grant said. And after a moment he added, "She had no stamina, anyway."

He took up the book again. She sat quietly watching him. He read well, his voice warm and sympathetic, his eyes kindling and kind. Watching him, she thought, "I know exactly how Mr. Seabury felt. Grant is like that, too. If he loved me I could trust him to my last breath. He'd hurt me over and over, but I'd always trust him."

It was one night in her room that she first thought of it—of how to make Grant see her. She had gone to a concert with Herbert Johnston, for whom she cared nothing at all. Grant had said, "I wish I were taking you to the concert, Elinor. But I don't feel like going out—just yet." She said, trying to be very light, "I've promised to go with Bert, anyway."

She searched his face, trying to see if he cared that she went with Bert.

But he only said very quietly, "Bert is a good fellow. I think I'll get those notes into final shape for the first half of the book, Elinor. The life seems to break quite sharply at the point where she first ran for public office, don't you think?"

"Yes," she said. "I'll be here in the morning at ten as usual."

He smiled down at her as he held her coat. "Good comrade," he said.

So she had sat all evening beside the thick, sturdy person of Bert Johnston, who was inheriting his father's solid business in a department store, and listened to a great violinist. The year was turning to spring and the windows of the auditorium were open. She could smell the fragrance of blossoms from the window near which they sat. The violin was singing and throbbing and she turned her head restlessly to gaze into the darkness beyond the window.

What did a woman do who loved a man who did not even see her? What did a nice woman do who loved a man like Grant? Grant was fastidious—a touch, a movement, a word that shocked his taste, and he would be repelled. How unequal love still was for men and women! There were women who might make love to men, women who might ask men even to marry them, but stronger than any such freedom was the fastidiousness of Grant—her own fastidiousness as well. It did not matter what other women did. She could do only what she was able to do. And she was not able to say boldly to Grant that she loved him. She would be ashamed all her life if she did.

The music deepened. Bert sighed and moved his knee and she shrank from him and went on thinking.

Grant did not even see her—that was the trouble. He saw no one—only that one woman who had been his mother. Until she could make him see someone else she could not discover whether or not he could love her. She was thinking very hard now, so hard that she did not any longer hear the music or remember where she was.

"Goodnight, Bert," she said at her own door. "Thank you so much."

He lingered, waiting. "It's not late," he said, and then he added with plain longing, "I don't see much of you these days, Elinor."

"I've been working rather hard," she said. "Grant and I are writing Mrs. Seabury's life."

"I see," he said slowly. "Well, goodnight."

"Goodnight," she said.

From his study her father's voice called, "Elinor, is that you?"

"Yes—coming!" she replied, and went in.

He was working over his collection of stamps. It was very large now and valuable and he never tired of it. "I have a new Indian stamp," he murmured.

She leaned over his shoulder and looked at a bit of saffron green paper upon which was printed a rajah's gold turbaned head.

"Odd," she said. She had never been interested in stamps. They seemed dead. She touched her father's cheek. "I'm going upstairs," she said.

"How was the music?" he asked, wanting to delay her.

"Perfect—almost," she replied.

"Almost?" he inquired.

"Oh well, Bert's not the companion for music," she said, laughing.

"Hm," said Mr. Brame. Then he said, "Elinor, have you noticed anything funny about Harry Seabury since Mrs. Seabury died?"

"No—what?" she asked.

"He's coming in late—or not at all. I don't want to fire

him—but it's queer. He's all dressed up, too, all the time."

"Is he?" she said, mystified. "No, I had not noticed."

"Well, notice sometime. Goodnight, my dear."

"Goodnight, Dad."

She went up to her room. Mr. Seabury—she mustn't forget to notice him. Then she forgot him at once. She opened her door and found the room full of moonlight. She went to the windowseat and sat down and leaned her chin on the palms of her hands. The only way to make Grant see her was to make him see his mother was dead—dead, buried, gone forever.

I'm going to hurry this whole business, she thought grimly. I've been letting him drag it out—he's living with her, that's what it is. He's not living in the world at all. It's outrageous.

She got up and put on the light and began to make ready for bed. She was not in the least sleepy, but it did not matter.

I'm going to kill Mrs. Seabury, she thought, climbing into bed and turning out the light. I'm going to kill her and bury her once and forever.

She lay a moment, motionless. The windows were wide open and the sweet spring air floated in like music.

She turned and buried her face in the pillows.

"Oh, *Grant!*" she cried, for a moment suffocating. Then she turned over again and lay still and straight, planning.

SHE WAS WORKING all day now, hurrying, hurrying to the end of Mrs. Seabury's life. They were now making the public figure Mrs. Seabury became when she was about forty. She and Grant had had one sharp disagreement before that. It was over the question of Mrs. Seabury's marriage. There were a few pages in the diary after her marriage when the picture of Mrs. Seabury became quite obscure. That is, what Mrs. Seabury had then written seemed shyly out of character. There was mention, for instance, of apple trees in bloom and a canoe ride on the river. "Harry has a lovely disposition," she wrote. "He says such funny things, too, that I can see how he has so many friends. I am very happy. I am coming to see that marriage is a good thing. Our home is very pleasant. Harry is working very hard. Just now I am much occupied in arranging and organizing the house. Later I shall hope to have time for other details. I believe that women have civic duties from which marriage does not excuse them. Just at present, however, my time seems quite full. I am studying Harry's tastes in food, games, reading, and so forth. I am determined to be a successful wife. I have bought several books on the subject, including one on the more intimate aspects. I must confess I feel uncomfortable in reading this book, and not for the world would I have Harry see it. But I feel there are things I should know. I do so want Harry to be happy."

"Last night," she wrote again, "the moon was full. Harry and I sat together on the porch until almost midnight. The content which filled me amazed me. I fear I am living a very idle life. It must not continue."

Then she wrote later, "We were at a small dance tonight at the country club—young married people. It was the first time we had gone out together. I took pains to be pleasant to my partners. But I saw Harry laughing very much with a newcomer to the town, a little Mrs. Cassels. She is a small, dark type—very pretty, to be just to her. She talked gaily and constantly. Later when Harry and I danced, I could think of nothing new to say except to tell him the town council had passed the measure for the new civic center. I suppose I should read more light books and novels. Just at present, however, I am reading an excellent work on town planning which is very interesting. I cannot escape the conviction that life should not be lived for pleasure."

Grant said eagerly, "I must make a note of that, Elinor. It was the beginning of her interest in the planned town."

"Oh, the poor thing!" Elinor cried softly.

"What do you mean?" he asked.

She had the diary and her eyes ran ahead to a sentence. He came over to her and she pointed to it.

"I asked Harry when we came home whether he liked women who were dark or fair. I cannot imagine why this seemed of importance to me, but it did. He replied that if I meant Mrs. Cassels, he thought she was pretty. I could not forget this for a time—until, in fact, I brought my reason to bear upon it. Mrs. Cassels is a married woman and Harry is a married man. It does not matter what he thinks of her. I was able to dismiss the matter at last from my mind."

From then on there was no more mention of Mrs. Cassels, and Mrs. Seabury began to take up town planning in earnest.

"We must put that glimpse of her in," Elinor said, "—that wistful, timid woman, wanting to learn how to be gay—for his sake."

"No," Grant said, "it's not like her."

"Yes, it is, Grant," she argued.

"It's not worthy of what she really was," he replied. "Besides, you mustn't forget—this book is for the public—for the thousands of people who look up to her, and want to look up to her. If we put in a thing like that, it isn't fair to her. She overcame every weakness in herself. What we have to show is the woman she really was."

"You're wrong," she cried, "you're very wrong, Grant! It's not fair to make her so perfect no one will believe in her at all. There must be a few faults or it will be only an effigy of her."

"I had rather burn all of this than stoop to discuss her faults," he answered rigidly. "She is my mother, Elinor."

They were staring hostilely at each other. It was she who gave way.

"Very well, Grant," she said.

She turned to the work again. How could a woman living and incomplete compete with a woman faultless in death?

"Now I begin to see her as I really knew her," Grant was saying exultantly. "Now she is beginning to be herself. I always see her as she was when I was about fifteen, before her hair turned gray. She grew even handsomer as she grew older. Her lines were good and she kept her figure. Do you remember that plum-colored velvet she had?"

"Yes," Elinor said.

"It made her look like a queen," he said, and his eyes were tender. "The first time she wore it was the night when she lectured to the women's clubs of the county. Do you remember?"

"No," Elinor said.

There was very little now in the diary about Harry Seabury—almost nothing, in fact, beyond an occasional mention that the business did not seem as prosperous as it had been when his father was alive—"due, perhaps," the diary said, "to general conditions. I try to think so, although reason compels me to see that Harry does not inherit all of his father's business acumen. I have offered to help, but Harry was offended, and I have said no more."

She became more absorbed than ever in civic affairs. A new hospital was built and she was on the board. The matter of a concentration of public schools came up and she carried on a fight for a consolidated high school and won it. It was about this time that Grant was born.

"People are asking me," Mrs. Seabury wrote, "whether I shall now give up public affairs. I say no, less than ever. For now I want to make the world a better place for my son to live in. I must simply organize my life better, so that I may fulfill all my obligations. . . . He looks like me, everyone says."

There was a space, and later, in blacker ink, she had written, "Grant is sitting alone! I have not written in my diary for a long time. I have discovered that a gang of scoundrels has been selling narcotics here in our city. It came out accidentally through the janitor at the hospital.

Mr. Cassels"—the name had been marked out, but they could see it under the ink—"a patient at the hospital was being supplied and no one could find out how. I took the matter in hand myself and suspected the janitor almost at once. He is a foreigner and has a bad face. I had noticed before, but I had said nothing, wishing to be just. I saw him coming out of a private room and when I asked him why he replied very rudely, 'He's a friend of mine.' Of course I knew the patient—a man of means—was not friendly with a janitor. The wretched janitor had discovered that at certain times the nurse was absent for meals."

She broke off to write, "Everything I do now has new meaning, since my son was born. He is an exceptionally fine child, Dr. Kenwood tells me. I spend a certain number of hours each day with him, allowing nothing to interfere."

Grant looked up. "Nothing ever interfered with her devotion to me—to home. Even when she went on her lecturing tours, in later years, she'd plan our menus for every meal while she was gone."

"That's in one of the letters," Elinor murmured. They had had dozens of letters from women who had written when they heard there was to be a biography of Ethel Seabury by her son, to tell him of what they remembered of his distinguished mother.

"I well remember," a letter said, "the day when dear Mrs. Seabury was at our club. We were at luncheon, and she had been discussing the new child labor law—she was to speak on that afterward—and suddenly she stopped, and a lovely, gentle look came over her fine, strong face, and she said, 'Half-past one, Wednesday— my dear ones are having at this moment broiled chops, peas, and braised tomatoes—and they are going to have apple pie and cheese—they love apple pie!' We all laughed, but we loved her for it. She was *wonderful!*"

She despaired as the work went on. For day by day Mrs. Seabury grew into sounder reality. Grant was writing now page upon page of the final book. He wrote well, at once compactly and fluently, and devotion glowed through the lines. He was making a thing he loved. Each day he read aloud to Elinor what he had written and she watched a glorified Mrs. Seabury emerging more and more clearly. Perhaps it was going to be harder to kill this shining figure than it had been for death to take the flesh-and-blood one. She struggled against its inhuman perfection.

"Grant, we must make her human, you know, or people won't believe in her at all."

"I don't know what you mean," he said. "I am simply putting down what I know was true."

He was right, in a way. Everything he put down was true. Mrs. Seabury was forgetful of herself, she was large in mind, tireless in her work. She had a gift for knowing what were the real issues in any situation, national and international, and she could present them simply and clearly, so that everybody could understand the right and wrong. She was absolutely honest, wholly fearless— oblivious, indeed, to danger, when she had decided upon a course. Why, then, perversely did Elinor secretly want to put in certain things that were not in the diary—such things, for instance, as her never being able to see a joke? She remembered Mrs. Seabury's tolerant smile when other people were roaring over a joke. She remembered Mrs. Seabury coming to call, once, before her own mother died. She and her mother were out in the garden, spraying the French lilacs.

"Oh dear," her mother had whispered when Fanny came to tell them Mrs. Seabury was in the parlor. "Tell her to come out here." And when Mrs. Seabury had come out, her mother asked, "What do you do for scale on your lilacs, Mrs. Seabury?" And Mrs. Seabury said, very simply and without meaning to be unpleasant, "I have no time for flowers, Mrs. Brame. There are so many more important things to do."

"Oh dear," her mother said, "I suppose there are."

For a while Elinor had hated Mrs. Seabury for the sober look that came over her mother's face. But it was impossible really to hate Mrs. Seabury. For she said, ponderingly, "I could ask Mrs. Gregg in Cincinnati what to do about that scale, Mrs. Brame. Her husband is a florist." And a month or two later there arrived four typed pages on lilac scale, with a short note from Mrs. Seabury.

That was the year, too, when Mrs. Seabury had organized the Community Chest so well that there was not a home beyond Third Street that did not have a turkey for Christmas. Still, Mrs. Seabury had not liked it when her mother would not serve on the committee.

"Oh dear, no," her mother had said, laughing. "I haven't the slightest gift for that sort of thing."

"It is a matter of duty," Mrs. Seabury had said a little grimly, but still gently.

"Oh, I never pay any attention to my duty," her mother replied flippantly. Her mother was always so flippant with Mrs. Seabury—much more flippant than she really was. She wanted to cry out to Mrs. Seabury, "My mother's *good*—she's always giving things to poor people." But she did not dare. If she had, her mother would have denied it and flouted the very idea.

"Oh, Nellie, I don't!" she would have cried. "I only

throw away old things I don't want. I don't care who picks them up."

So she had said nothing, and after Mrs. Seabury had gone away her mother had seized her madly in her arms and squeezed her and cried, "Promise me, darling, you'll never—never—never be a wonderful woman!"

"I promise!" she had squeaked, quite breathless.

It was true one could not put such things into the book. They were such intangible things, fading away so quickly before the solid reality of Mrs. Seabury's League for the Political Education of Women. Besides, there was really no self-righteousness about Mrs. Seabury. Everyone had been surprised and a little shocked when she talked against prohibition. She was so exactly the sort of person everybody thought would believe in it. But no, she said, "Prohibition is, in the first place, unconstitutional. I hate liquor, but more than liquor, I hate infringement of personal liberty. Besides, people are going to get the stuff if they want it."

Nevertheless, after the law was passed, she obeyed it rigidly, and until it was repealed, she never allowed a drop of alcohol in her house. It was of course a little disconcerting to a hostess to have her refuse a cocktail.

"No, thanks—I don't touch it on principle," she always said quietly. People had to respect her, although it spoiled the cocktails for everyone else, however determined one was not to show it.

So Grant went on making the book.

Whether or not she could ever have killed Mrs. Seabury without help she did not know. But just as Mrs. Seabury was reaching the height of her career during World War II, when she went to Washington and devoted her entire time to the food conservation program, one morning Rhodes tapped at the door.

They had just read what Mrs. Seabury had said in the diary about the war. "Since my son is not old enough for me to give him to our great cause," she had written, "I must give myself." She did not mention her husband here, although a few pages before she had noted baldly, "Harry has had to go through bankruptcy. I have agreed to lend him ten thousand dollars of the money my father left me, which I had hoped to put into trust entire for Grant."

Rhodes opened the door and coughed. He looked in consternation at Grant and whispered, "He's here again, sir."

Grant knew instantly who it was.

"It's Peter," he said grimly to Elinor. Then his look changed. It was at this moment that Elinor saw a new Grant, a timid, shrinking, horrified boy.

"Let me see what he wants," she said quickly.

"No, no," Grant said. He straightened himself. "No, I couldn't let you. It's my business to—I'll just do what Mother would do." He wet his lips. "Show him in, Rhodes. But if he asks for whiskey and soda, don't give it to him."

"No, sir," Rhodes replied. His face wore the pitying air of the superior servant.

So Peter came in.

"Well, well, well, my boy!" he shouted. He was a large man and very stout, and his face had the crude color and the metallic brightness of one who habitually drank heavily. He was dressed in a shabby dark blue suit and he had no overcoat, but a new red silk scarf was tucked around his neck. He held out both hands to Grant, pudgy, stiff-fingered hands, dry and rough.

"Hello," Grant said coldly. Peter turned instinctively away from this coldness.

"Who's this?" he asked heartily, staring at Elinor. "You look familiar—we haven't met somewhere, have we?"

He was pulling out the scarf now and rolling it in a wad and stuffing it into his pocket. His eyes were very bright blue, and although rascal was written in every line of his face, Elinor could not keep from smiling at him.

"No," she answered. "I know who you are, though. Grant's told me."

"*He* don't know me," Peter shouted gaily. He sat down by the fire and drew up his very tight trousers slightly. Above his old shoes his socks drooped. "Grant's not spoken to me in years, have you, Grant? No, I always did business with Ethel. Say, Grant, I just came to tell you I was awfully sorry to see the news about her. Saw it in the Chicago *Tribune.* I'd have come to the funeral, if I'd had the price of a ticket, but I was low, then. Money's been my misfortune—Miss—Miss—"

"Brame," Elinor said. Grant evidently would not introduce her. He was sitting by the table, looking over the pages he had written. His face was set. Peter laughed and leaned toward her, his fat hands on his knees.

"Say," he whispered in a wheeze, "it was the funniest thing, but when I saw that notice my first thought was to telegraph Ethel for the money—you know—to come to her funeral! I couldn't realize it."

A paper knife fell to the floor.

"What do you want now?" Grant demanded. He was looking at Peter as though he were filth with which he would not be defiled.

"Nothing," said Peter airily, "not a thing. Just looked in. Family interest, that's all. Well, there is one little thing I could mention—a sure thing this time, Grant— nothing like anything I've ever done before. But I'll tell you about it later." He looked around the room. "It's queer not to see Ethel—seems as if she must be here. I was fond of Ethel. I never forgot she was my sister."

"You might as well tell me what you came for," Grant said in a stifled voice.

Peter coughed. "Yes, well, maybe you're right," he said. He took a gray handkerchief out of his pocket and wiped his lips. "Well, Grant, I'll tell you—I've got hold of the swellest comedy Broadway's ever seen. It's a knockout, it's a wow, it's a scream, it's got swing and wit and everything else."

Grant interrupted him. "You know there's no more use in your coming to me about this sort of thing than there was to come to my mother."

"Well now, you're a young chap," Peter argued. His eyes were snapping. "I said to myself, Ethel, she could hardly be expected—she never was much for amusements even when she was a girl. But—"

"I'm not interested in that sort of amusement," Grant said. He was taking some bills out of his pocket and putting them in an envelope as he talked and he pushed the envelope toward Peter. "I'm not a gambler and I'm not interested in comic shows."

"I don't want your money, Grant," Peter protested briskly. "I said I came here because I wanted to show family interest and I did. Now that Ethel's gone, I wanted you to know I didn't have any hard feelings." He rose and pulled the red scarf out of his pocket and began knotting it around his neck. "She used to tell me pretty regularly what she thought of me," he went on and laughed a little. "Well, I never contradicted her. She was right. Besides, she always helped me along a little. Her bark was worse than her bite—that was Ethel." He paused and stared at Elinor. "Say," he said suddenly,

"you look kind of like Ethel yourself, young lady—like
her when she was your age, of course. She was tall, too,
and light and had gray eyes. Only you look as though
you could laugh. She couldn't. Well, so long, Grant.
Your dad and I are eating together. I'm to meet him at
the bank. 'I won't come in,' I told him, 'I'll just wait
ouside.' Lord, it would scare me to go into a bank—a
bank's no use to me, nor I to it." He wheezed out his
tight laughter and nodded at Grant and held out his hand
to her. She took it, liking him somehow. "Yep," he said,
"you're like Ethel!" He gave her hand a great shake and
was gone.

"You see he took the money," Grant said dryly.

The envelope was not on the table.

"I can't imagine why he goes on like this," Grant said
in a low voice. "He's never been any use to anyone.
Mother told me once that even when she was a girl she
always felt responsible for him. It made her old even
then. She couldn't be really lighthearted, because he was
always disgracing them—he wouldn't study, and he ran
away to New York and got interested in the stage—in
silly shows."

"Didn't he ever have a success?" Elinor asked.

"You see him," Grant said curtly. "He spent his
money as fast as he got it. When a show did pretty
well—he used to say they did, sometimes—he'd waste
everything on parties and foolishness."

She watched his handsome, frowning face and did not
speak.

"And he even got my father to thinking there was
something to it," he went on. "I don't know where we'd
have been if Mother hadn't just refused to let them have
a bit of money. It was the last time when Dad failed and
he didn't want to go into the bank." He sighed and

added, "Oh, well, let's forget Peter. I gave him enough to stay away a while."

He suddenly looked so much like his mother that she felt repelled.

"I rather thought Peter was fun," she said perversely. "I rather liked him."

Grant was gathering up the scattered pages.

"You wouldn't think so if he were your uncle," he said. His voice was so superior, so detached from her, that her perverseness rose to a flicker of anger.

"I'm not a snob," she said carelessly. "I shouldn't mind."

"Elinor!" he said sharply. "What do you mean?"

He was looking at her, his eyebrows lifted and his mouth cold. She shrugged her shoulders.

"I like Peter, that's all. I may like him, mayn't I?"

"Certainly," Grant said. He turned away from her and began counting the pages. "After all, he paid you a great compliment. He said you looked like Mother."

He looked up at her. Then he stared at her, and his voice came strained and strange. "I never thought of it," he said, "but you do look like her—a little." He dropped the papers in his hand and came toward her. "Why, Elinor," he said excitedly, "did anyone ever tell you that before? I feel as if I were seeing you for the first time."

She could not bear it. She could not bear it that he was seeing her now like this because he imagined there was a look about her of his mother. She lifted her head.

"I don't want to look like anyone," she said. "I am only myself."

"My mother was handsome enough for any woman to be proud to look like her," Grant said, astonished, "and you ought to be proud."

"I'm not," she said. The flicker of anger was growing

to a flame. It was licking about her heart, consuming every shred of caution, of patience, of the humility which she had had to learn because she loved Grant. It was all gone in a mounting blaze of anger. If there were only ashes afterward, let there be ashes. She rose suddenly and picked up her hat and gloves from a chair and turned away.

"What's the matter?" he asked.

She did not speak, but she was going to speak. She was planning how to do it all at once. She put on her hat and she fitted on the fingers of her gloves. Then she said distinctly, "I'm tired of your mother. You can finish the book yourself. I've done all I can on it, anyway. And I tell you, I'm sick and tired of your mother. I was tired of her years ago." She wanted to say, "Everybody was," but she could not quite say that to Grant.

She turned toward the door without looking at him.

"No, but Elinor!" He was coming after her. "You can't go away like this—besides, how can you say you're tired of Mother? She was wonderful to you!"

"She's dead," Elinor said. She paused at the door and faced him. Now she had stabbed Mrs. Seabury, and she would stab her again. "She's dead and gone. Besides, I was wonderful to her, too."

She pushed the door open and without once looking back at him, she walked out of the house into the middle of the summer's day. She had killed Mrs. Seabury at last.

Her car was swirling down a dusty country road.

"Where are you going?" he had shouted at her as she flew down the steps of his house.

"Where you can't find me!" she had shouted back. She was half sobbing as she drove headlong down the street.

A policeman saw her and roared at her but she did not stop. She must get away somewhere, anywhere, where Grant could not find her.

"I'm a fool!" she cried to herself. The wind caught the words and crammed them down her throat. "Hanging around waiting for him—wasting my life—I've wasted years on Grant and he doesn't know I'm alive. I don't know why I love him—he's so like his mother!"

It was summer, midsummer—a year and a half since Mrs. Seabury's funeral, but for Grant it might have been yesterday.

I give up, she thought bitterly. The speedometer shot up another five miles and she did not notice it. She had not the slightest idea of where she would go to leave Grant, but she drove on into the afternoon, angrily glad for every mile that grew between them. Miles and miles, the more the better. She went on for hours, brooding and reckless. The hot afternoon sunshine was growing golden with evening and the trees threw elongated shadows across the road, but she went on, heedless of the time until she chanced to see the gas meter. The tank was almost empty. She must stop as soon as she could. And then, slowing down a little, she felt herself very weary with the weak fatigue that comes from inner strain.

She saw a small station and pulled up. The road had grown narrow and winding and hills rose closely around. A slatternly woman came out when she blew the horn.

"Twelve," Elinor said shortly.

"You must of come a long way," the woman said. "Christ!" she sighed as she waited, "I wisht I cud go somewheres. I don't do nothin' but set here and git gas for other people to go."

"Why do you stay if you don't want to stay?" Elinor

asked listlessly. She did not care, but one had to say something.

"My man's had a fall," the woman said. "He's all crippled up." She paused and eased the lever. "He says to me, 'Go on, take a vacation, kid.' I says to him, ' 'Twouldn't be no vacation. I'd be thinking about you all the time and it'd be the same thing as draggin' you along.' No, I've tied myself, I guess."

Elinor counted out the money. "Thanks," she said.

"Thank *you*," the woman said.

She drove on in late sunlight, but now more slowly. She was taking her body farther and farther from Grant, that was all. She had not for one moment stopped thinking of him. No, the farther she went the more deeply she knew that she was taking him with her. The evening was windless and hot and the rushing air was burning on her face. There was no one to be seen. Around her were the pressing hills, and ahead the empty road, going on and on. There was peace of a sort, but there was intense loneliness, too. Perhaps the two went always together. What the slatternly woman had said so accidentally had come like the voice of life. One tied oneself. She could never really leave Grant.

I've tied myself, she thought. She pulled her car to the side of the road, and sat for a long time thinking. She was sorting out her life and there was only one pattern possible. She must go back to Grant—if he never loved her, then she must go on loving him, living near him, sharing humbly what he would allow her to share. She turned slowly about at last and went back over the road along which she had come.

It was long past midnight when she reached home. The house was lighted from top to bottom. She pulled up and stumbled from her car, up the steps. In the shadows there were other cars, but she was too tired to look at them. She wanted only to go upstairs, to be alone, to sleep, having accepted her own bondage. She loved Grant and she would always love him.

I suppose I'll have to spend my life like this, she thought dully.

She opened the door. There were voices in the living room, and she paused a moment, listening. She was too tired for company. She would go upstairs and send a maid down to her father. But her father was saying agitatedly, "I'll wait one more hour, that's all. Then we'll call the police."

"Wait—" She heard Peter's blurred voice. "She wasn't the kind harm would come to . She can manage herself. No, she's made up her mind to something."

"I agree to that," Mr. Seabury's voice said. "Elinor's got sense."

A light, high voice broke in. "I *don't* know her, of course, but if she was anything like her mother, she's just—gone away. Dear Mr. Brame, it was your wife who gave me courage to run away from Tony Cassels. I'll never, *never* be able to thank her enough. I was so disturbed at last that I went to see her because she always seemed so happy. And she said, 'Why do you stay if you don't like it?' So simple, wasn't it?—and so very true. I've been so grateful all these years. That's why I said when the news came—I was having dinner with Peter, wasn't I, Peter?—we're terribly old friends—I said, 'If it's that dear little Mrs. Brame's daughter'—so we came on—Mr. Seabury was dining with us—he's a terribly old friend, too. So when Grant telephoned—you don't mind my saying Grant, do you?"

"I can't think—I don't know—" her father broke in. "What do you think, Grant?"

Grant! But she did not hear Grant's voice. She went

the few steps to the door and looked in. Yes, Grant was there. He was sitting by the big table, his head on his hand.

"Well, who's this!" Peter cried loudly.

"It's I," she said faintly and felt herself smile at them foolishly.

They looked up. No, she saw only Grant look up. He leaped to his feet.

"Elinor!" he said. That was all. But she saw his eyes, his seeing eyes. For the first time in her life they were upon her. She swayed a little.

"Elinor, you're ill!" Her father hurried to her. She felt his arm over her shoulder.

"Why, the dear child's fainting," Mrs. Cassels's bright voice rang out.

But she was not listening to them. No, she wanted to stay forever in the light of Grant's eyes. He had leaped to his feet. He was beside her, commanding them all. "Elinor, come upstairs—straight to bed. Mr. Brame, she ought to have something hot."

"Toddy," said Peter cheerfully. "I have a toddy guaranteed—"

They were all hurrying to her. She felt Grant's arm around her and she clung to him and hid her eyes.

"How could you, Elinor!" he was whispering. "How could you, my darling!"

"I don't know," she murmured. "I don't know. I suppose I was insane." She smiled, her eyes half shut. "Fit to be tied, maybe," she murmured. The old homely phrase was warm on her lips. Her mother used to say that. "Fit to be tied—" she repeated.

She was so tired. Now that she was clinging to Grant she was desperately tired. In a haze she heard his voice guiding, directing. He was leading her upstairs. Now they were in her room.

Grant was saying, "Mrs. Cassels, if you will have the maid draw a hot bath—and you might just stay and see that she gets into bed—safely. No, Mr. Brame, I don't believe she needs a doctor. I think I know—not a toddy, Peter, if you please—much better have hot milk. I'll wait downstairs until she is in bed."

Through the mists she murmured, "Grant, don't go away."

"Never," he said firmly. "Besides, " he added, "wasn't it you who went away from me? Don't ever do it again."

He was putting her on the chaise longue, and now he was taking off his shoes.

"You can't argue with me," she murmured happily. "I'll agree to anything—now."

"I'll just make a note of that," he said. He was laughing a little. "Someday I'll want to refer to it, maybe— someday when we've been married a long, long time, and you get stubborn, maybe."

She woke up suddenly from her daze. He was asking her to marry him! She wanted to cry, but she smiled.

"There's no use pretending I won't marry you," she said lightly.

"Not a bit," he agreed. He kissed her quickly while Mrs. Cassels was bustling into the bathroom with towels.

"Nice," Elinor murmured. There were tears in her eyes and she hid them with her eyelids.

"What?" he asked.

"Sense of humor," she whispered. "I believe you have one, after all. I couldn't marry you otherwise." In her breast her heart cried out to her, "Liar! You'd marry him anyway!"

"THERE'S SOMETHING ELSE amazing," Elinor said. It was only August and they were on the terrace above the garden.

"Everything is," he agreed.

"No, but I mean finding that the person you're marrying really *is*, you know—much better even than the one you fell in love with and had been sort of in love with always."

"Yes, isn't it!" he agreed again.

His eyes were smiling upon her. She hadn't known before that Grant's eyes could smile like that.

"Your eyes didn't used to smile before your mother died," she said suddenly.

That was another amazing thing. She had been able to tell Grant everything she felt about Mrs. Seabury at last. At first she thought, He'll be hurt if I tell him— and still she felt she must tell him, because she couldn't go on being hypocritical, pretending to join in a worship she did not feel. The book was all written. Nothing she could say would change that. She did not want to change it. The fine statue was made, so let it stand. No, but Grant must know how she felt inside. So almost at once she told him everything—how when Mrs. Seabury saw her that day at the country club, dressed for her first dance, she had said, "I cannot understand the present custom of painting the face—" That was all. She had not mentioned the new gown of rosy tissue.

"She had an uncanny way of hurting one's wretched little vanity," Elinor said. "Of course I know she never used rouge herself. No, but she should have remembered that I scarcely ever did—and forgiven me for my first party. She was so inflexible, Grant."

He took this wonderfully well. "I suppose she was," he said, reflecting. "I didn't see it before."

"Why do you see it now?" she asked.

"I suppose—because of you," he said. "I see you."

"You wouldn't want to change the book?" she asked.

He shook his head. "No," he said, "no, she was that to me."

"Not anymore?" she pressed him.

"Yes," he said, "to remember. But that awful afternoon and night—do you remember what your last words to me were?"

She nodded. "I felt I had killed her for you."

"In a way you did," he answered. "At least, I saw at last that she was dead, and you—you were living."

She was so happy she was still dazed with it. The night was moonless, soft and black. She was glad of the darkness so that she could only feel Grant's arm about her, feel his hand about hers, hear his voice. She was closer to him because she could only feel and not see. There was so much she needed to feel beneath Grant's dignity of form and bearing which his mother had given him. She was learning that underneath there were passion and impatience—things which Mrs. Seabury had not made. She had taught him to hold himself straight and aloof, to speak calmly, to reason coolly. But Mrs. Seabury had driven deep into the caverns of his being this something else that was Grant, too, this something else which she had dimly felt and always loved, and which he had not showed his mother.

Ah, he was impatient: he would not wait at all for their marriage. It was she who had made him wait.

"You have to finish the book first," she had insisted.

"But why?" he had demanded.

"Because," she had said willfully, "you can't think about anything but me after we're married." She was very daring now that Mrs. Seabury was really dead. "I won't have you thinking about any other woman," she said positively.

It was so delightful to be willful with him, to insist and tease and play at being imperious with this lordly Grant, that she could not forbear. And especially when she saw him growing more subject to her every day. She had been docile so long she enjoyed being a little imperious now.

There was the day, for instance, when they had had the great argument over where they should live.

"I wish we could live in my house. I wish we didn't have to go back to my job," Grant had said.

She shook her head. "I couldn't," she said, instantly. "No."

"But—" he began.

"It's no use," she said in the gayest and firmest of voices. "I couldn't live in your mother's house. I'd be haunted."

"Oh, nonsense!" he cried.

"Yes, I would," she repeated. "Yes, I would—yes, I would—yes, I would—"

He seized her and kissed her ruthlessly. She struggled a little away.

"Besides," she said, "there'd be Peter—it looks as if he isn't going away."

Peter had moved into the room next to Mr. Seabury's, for a night, and had stayed. "Just temporary, that's all, until I get my business going," he had said airily. "Gosh, this show I want to back up—it's a wonderful show—a young fellow I know wrote about an old fellow dreamin' his life over again, the way he might have lived it. Gosh, I cried just reading it!"

Grant looked grave and his arm dropped. "I don't understand it," he said irritably. "It's ridiculous—he and Dad starting together—and such a business!" He lit a cigarette. "You must admit it was wise of Mother, anyway, to leave Dad's share of her money in trust. Look what would have happened—he'd have sunk it all in this ridiculous theatrical stuff."

For Mr. Seabury had promised to back the play—no, more than Mr. Seabury—Peter and Mrs. Cassels and Mr. Seabury. It was absurd, and she had laughed and laughed.

"They're having so much fun," she said.

"Where they will get the money—" Grant had frowned. "Unless it's that Mrs. Cassels—"

She did not tell him what they had told her. For they had told her everything. They were three irresponsible young things, aged forty-five to forty-eight.

"I never say I'm older than forty," Mrs. Cassels had tinkled.

"Why should you? It wouldn't be true!" Peter the gallant had said, and had kissed her hand ceremoniously.

They had scraped up bits of money here and there. Mrs. Cassels had a little and she had thrown it recklessly in and had mortgaged her alimony besides. Peter had nothing, of course. But he had friends.

"I couldn't ask them for myself," he declared with grandeur. "But this is different—it's a sure thing—it's genius."

They went back and forth to New York in whirls of

excitement. As yet no one would produce the play.

"I'll produce it myself!" Peter had roared.

"I don't know what's the matter with people of Dad's generation," Grant said. His handsome face was severe with disgust. "They simply won't mature decently. I'm glad Mother can't see it."

In the plain living room of Mrs. Seabury's house certain nonsensical things had appeared, for instance, a foolish cushion for Mrs. Cassels's back.

"There simply isn't a comfortable chair in this house," she had complained prettily. "My feet won't reach the floor anywhere."

So there were some silly footstools. And her little lace handkerchiefs were dropped everywhere, looking as strange and unwelcome as moths in Mrs. Seabury's house. Mrs. Cassels lived at the hotel. She had come from New York just for a few days, because of Peter, and to see the old town.

"I've a sweet apartment there in New York," she said, but she did not go back to it. She stayed on and on. "I'm having such fun," she said every day.

"God, speaking of women, how there can be such women as that Mrs. Cassels!" Grant said abruptly now in the darkness. "You can say what you like about Mother—when I see a woman like that Cassels creature—"

"Oh, of course," Elinor said quickly. He turned to her and she felt his smooth, hard cheek against her lips.

"If I hadn't found you," he whispered, "I'd have been lost after she went."

"I really was there all the time, though," she murmured against his cheek.

"No!" he cried, squeezing her a little, pretending to be surprised.

"Yes, I was!" she insisted.

"I didn't see you," he exclaimed.

"I know you didn't," she murmured. "You wouldn't look at me." Her face was pressed into his neck.

"Why didn't you tell me?" he demanded.

"You didn't ask me," she replied, and laughed. "Silly!" she added.

Then, in the hiding darkness, she told him all about it—how she had loved him and loved him. And he was humbled and ashamed.

"Oh, Elinor—sweet—" He wrapped her in his arms. "We're going in a house of our own—where nobody's ever been except you and me—where there will never be anybody else."

"Yes," she cried, "yes, yes—"

They bought a small, exceedingly comfortable house on the edge of the town where he taught in the university. It stood back from the street and no other houses were very near. It was quite new. No one had ever lived in it. There were no ghosts at all. And Mrs. Seabury had never even seen it.

They were married one day at the end of August, very quietly, in her old home in the living room. She thought once of Mrs. Seabury while she stood beside Grant, making her promises, and that was all. If Grant thought of his mother—no, Grant did not think of Mrs. Seabury. She felt no coldness of a shadow anywhere. If Mrs. Seabury had come in, there would have been a coldness. And there was none.

Her father was wistful for a moment when she came downstairs in her green suit to go away, but it was a warm wistfulness.

"You don't look like your mother usually," he said, "but there's something about you just at this moment that reminds me of her."

She kissed him. "I shall be coming back and forth," she said calmly.

There was a moment of Peter and Mrs. Cassels.

"Brides are so sweet!" Mrs. Cassels cried. "Oh, do be happy, child!"

"I'll see you sometime—when the show's started," Peter promised.

Afterward she said to Grant, "Your father was as quiet as anything." Mr. Seabury had stood, his head a little to one side, watching her.

"I don't know what's the matter with him these days," Grant said. "He's been like that—doesn't even play the flute anymore."

They forgot him. He was a ghost, too, and he faded from them. No one mattered for them. The new house was warm and waiting and empty and they went into it and began to live.

Grant, at work, was quite another person. She was a little awed by him as an assistant professor, and rather a popular one. She had to grow used to hearing the doorbell ring very hard and to discovering on her doorstep young men who blushed brilliantly and wanted to know where Professor Seabury was. That, of course, was Grant.

"Come in," she said, smiling. "He's in his study. I'll call him."

"Oh, don't trouble him," they always said while they stumbled into the house. "If he hasn't time—" and while they said this they were swarming into her long, lovely living room and sinking into her satin cushions and wiping their dusty feet on her new rugs.

But she did not mind. It was so pleasant to see Grant come in. She always pretended she hadn't seen him before. Then she could see him come in freshly, keen and interested and eager.

"Oh, Professor Seabury," they began, "we just wanted to ask you—"

"Yes?" he answered in his kind, strong voice. He never tired of doing for them. He always answered them patiently and fully, though she knew he had counted on this hour to correct his freshman themes. There was a sort of tireless goodness in him that never failed. It upheld him and it wore him out. For this goodness was, she felt, sometimes, a tyrant. It would not let him rest. He could never take his ease. She learned not to persuade him to stay at home from faculty meetings, for instance.

It had been a sort of game, at first. She would pretend that she would be too lonely if he went. She clung about his neck and implored him.

"Oh, Grant, please, please, don't leave me!"

He loosened her arms. "But, my darling, I must. It's my duty."

"They don't expect you every time."

"That's not the point." He had her arms down from his neck and he was holding her hands.

"Mrs. Jamieson says Professor Jamieson regularly goes only every other time."

He put down even her hands. "That has nothing to do with me," he replied.

Was there a ghost in this house? There was a look on his face that made her think of something she had seen before, on another face. She turned away quickly.

"Of course you must go. I understand," she said slowly.

His face took on its anxious look. "Perhaps I'm wrong. Perhaps—I am away too much."

Oh, she was afraid of ghosts. She freed herself to laugh.

"Oh, silly darling, no! I was just making love to you. Of course you must go. Besides, I have a new book. I'll be perfectly happy!"

"I only want to do my duty, sweet."

Oh, go away, ghost! Mrs. Seabury's handsome, frowning face, anxious, pondering. Mrs. Seabury saying, "I only want to do my duty—"

"Go on, darling—here's your hat—here's your pipe—"

"Sure you're all right?"

"Sure—sure—sure—"

And in the house alone she breathed deeply. The ghost was gone. She looked out the window. For a moment she seemed to see a tall faithful mist floating behind him.

Silly! she thought. She turned on all the lights and took up her new book and read resolutely. Long before she expected him, he was back. She heard the door open and looked up startled to see him rushing to her. He was kneeling before her and his arms were about her.

"Why, why—" she said, half laughing.

"I'm such a fool," he said. "I got thinking about you sitting here all alone. And there wasn't anything of importance at the meeting—old routine stuff. So I rose and left."

"Oh, Grant, *ought* you?" she whispered.

"Don't talk about *ought* to me," he said passionately.

She slipped from her chair into his arms and felt his deep kiss. Of course there were no ghosts.

No, but one rainy Sunday morning she was polishing the silver teapot that had been her mother's. Sunday was a lovely day, for Grant did no work at all. However high his desk was piled with the endlessly mounting themes, on Sunday she knew he would not open the door to them. They slept late and came downstairs late to breakfast on what they liked best to eat. And after breakfast he did not hurry away. He sat over a book, smoking, and she did whatever she wanted to do, where he was. This morning it was the teapot. She had noticed last week that the knobby roses of its design were black in the creases. Dillie, their maid, did not take creases seriously. So she had brought the pot into the living room and spread a newspaper on the floor at Grant's feet and settled herself with her brushes and polishes and chamois skin. He threw a fresh log on the fire and leaned over to kiss her.

And at that moment they saw Mrs. Benton coming up the walk.

"Oh, Grant!" Elinor moaned. She made a face toward Mrs. Benton.

"Can't be helped," Grant said briefly.

The doorbell rang twice, loudly and firmly, and he went to open the door. Elinor gathered up the newspaper, polishes, pot, everything, and took them into the dining room. If it had been Mrs. Petrie, the president's wife, she would have gone on with the teapot. Everybody loved Mrs. Petrie, though there was no use in pretending she made a good president's wife. She had once been a singer and she still sang in a lovely, big, loose contralto voice. But she never bothered about meetings or receptions. So that was why Mrs. Benton, the dean's wife, had to. She had to do all the things Mrs. Petrie should have done. At least that was what everyone said, and Mrs. Benton said so, too.

She'll want me to do something, Elinor thought. She'd never come to see me if she didn't.

She went in, though, as she had to, and shook Mrs. Benton's hand and said brightly, "What a morning—you're a brave woman, Mrs. Benton."

The rain was turning to icy sleet and it was driving in

little tinkling darts against the windows. Mrs. Benton loosened her black cloth coat.

"I didn't dare put if off a day," she said. She had a curious, flat, toneless voice, always too loud. "It's shamefully late now for the reception to the new students. We're planning it for Thursday, and I wondered if you wouldn't serve on my committee."

She opened her mouth to say what she had always said, what her mother had said before her, "Oh, I'm not the least good on committees." But she saw Grant's face. It had a certain look, a serious, intent, firm look. She closed her mouth and waited. Mrs. Benton went on.

"I know these tasks aren't very interesting. Dear me, no one knows it better than I do. I've been doing them for twenty-three years—lots of them not really the dean's wife's business to do at all. But somebody has to do them. I used to wait to see if they wouldn't be done. Now I've learned just to go ahead and do them and not wait for other people."

The atmosphere in the room changed. The carefree, leisurely peace became something tight. It was not Mrs. Benton who had done it. She could have coped with Mrs. Benton. She could have said, "Why bother about the reception, Mrs. Benton? I don't believe the new students like it any better that we do." And when Mrs. Benton said, as of course she would, "It's not what we *like*, it's what we *ought*," she would say— But Grant's face stopped all that. He knocked the ash sharply from his pipe.

"I think you ought to help, Elinor," he said. "It's rather important in the tradition of the college."

"Yes, isn't it?" Mrs. Benton said eagerly. "Well, thank you both *so* much. We're to meet tomorrow morning at eleven, at my house. I'd have telephoned, only I find it's so much easier for people to say *no* over the telephone." She stood up to button her heavy coat. "Of course if everybody would share the responsibility there wouldn't be so much for a few of us." She smiled bravely.

And after she was gone, Grant said restlessly, "I think I'll go and get on my clothes, Elinor. I really ought to get more exercise. The air will be good for me."

She might have said, "I'll go, too." But she did not.

"Very well, darling," she agreed. "I don't think I will, though."

"Good for you," he suggested, but she shook her head.

Alone, she went back to the living room and curled into Grant's chair. She was there when he came down a few moments later.

"Bye, sweet," he said, and kissed her quickly. A second later she saw through the window his tall figure striding through the sleet, head up, shoulders back. He'd be breathing deeply.

I suppose, she thought restlessly, I ought to go on and finish that teapot.

She half rose. Then she sat down again.

"I won't!" she said aloud to the ghost, and picked up a gay-backed magazine.

To her own dismay she had a good time on the committee. It was rather fun planning music, food, games. And it was very pleasant to have Grant approving her and listening and adding suggestions. When she had grown tired of making hundreds of little sandwiches she kept on doing it because of Grant's approval. She worked very hard during the reception under Grant's eyes. She looked up every now and then from her seat by the punch table, to meet his eyes. He was talking conscientiously to one new student after the other. And when it was nearly over and they were waiting for the students to stop eating and go away, Mrs. Petrie came rushing in, tall and rosy and blond, in a dark blue velvet dress, looking perfectly beautiful. Dr. Petrie had stood at the head of the reception line, very thin and a little stooped, shaking one hand after another, saying over and over again, "I'm so glad you are here. I hope this is the beginning of four happy years together," but Mrs. Petrie never came to receptions and people had stopped expecting it. And suddenly she was there, looking lovely, having done nothing at all, and someone begged her "Sing us something, Mrs. Petrie!" And the piano crashed into the gayest chords and her big voice rollicked out of the midst of the circle the students made about her.

At the table Mrs. Benton and a few faculty wives began setting things in order and piling up the dirty dishes. And Mrs. Benton whispered tightly, "That's always the way she does. They're crazy about her. But somebody's got to do the work, all the same."

When that night Elinor told this to Grant, he said instantly, "Of course Mrs. Benton is right." She did not answer. There was no use in answering ghosts.

How it all began it was difficult to remember, now that it was begun. Perhaps it had been that very reception.

She had somehow got in the habit of helping Grant to correct his papers. It was rather fun, too, reading the naive, ponderous young sentences. They were so earnest and so sure, and so touching.

"I don't know what I'd have done without you," he said.

Grant's approval was still the sweetest thing in the world. And so when Dean Benton wrote her a letter after midterms, asking if she would teach a freshman course in English composition, she said she would, merely because Grant said, "I believe you could manage it, darling—you're rather a capable young woman."

Almost immediately she found she hated the class, but she kept on at it because she was ashamed not to. How would she explain to Grant? She'd tell him in the summer, "I hate teaching, darling. I don't want to."

But in the early summer, the book about Mrs. Seabury was published. All year long there had been moments when the book had to be discussed, the type and the binding and the proofs. Grant said, "I want the book to look like Mother—solid and true and full of dignity." So they had chosen a plain dark blue cloth, stamped with gold letters, and the paper was white and not shining. Each time Elinor had felt distaste for the book, but she had not allowed it in herself. She had taken great pains.

And in the beginning of June the book was finished and off the press. She came home from a committee meeting on Commencement Day—Grant had said to her, "Of course you can do it, Elinor. You've a splendid head. Besides, I'd like to see things run more smoothly than they did last year"—and he met her at the door. There was a look on his face.

"Come and see," he said solemnly.

He led her into his study and there on his desk was the book, *Ethel Seabury: Her Life and Times*.

"Oh, Grant!" she said. "It looks just like her!"

"Doesn't it?" he said in his solemn voice. He took it lovingly, and she held back an impulse to take it from him. She turned away.

"I'm so glad it's finished, and just as you want it," she said.

"Don't you think it's just right?" he said. He was not

looking at her but at the book. His lips were tender and his eyes bright. "I wish she could see it."

"It's quite perfect," she said again. And then, cause-lessly, she was intensely weary. "If you don't mind, dar-ling," she began. He did not hear her. "I'm tired," she said. Her lips were trembling. "I'll go and wash and change."

He did not answer. Upstairs in her room she was sud-denly consumed with the old, stupid jealousy.

"I believe he still thinks she was the most wonderful woman in the world—"

She wept a little, since she was really very tired. Then she bathed and put on her old blue hostess gown and brushed her hair very hard and went downstairs and spent the evening with Grant and the book—and the ghost.

It was impossible after that to say to Grant that she wanted to give up teaching. He was reading the book over again, closely. "It's a good job," he said, when he had finished it. "But, then, how could it be otherwise? A life so vital, so full, so useful—it makes other women look like foolish children—except you."

"Oh, I'm nothing," she cried and made herself laugh when she had said it.

"You're beginning to do a number of things rather well, Elinor," he said seriously. "I've been noticing."

"Thank you!" She swept him a demure curtsey.

"No, I mean it," he insisted.

She bowed to him. But he did not see it. He was read-ing the dedication he had written in the book.

"To my mother, who alone has shown to me the beauty of goodness and of self-sacrifice."

So, mocking, she turned and bowed again, and this time to a ghost.

Still, all mockery aside, she could not give up the class now. So she put it out of her mind all summer and they went to Norway and Denmark and afterward to England and hurried back just in time for school. They debated whether or not they should go home for the two days before school opened.

"I'd rather like to see my dad," she said.

"We oughtn't to have done that extra bit in England," Grant said, frowning. "I have a lot to do before I'm ready."

She didn't feel she should interfere with his work. Besides, a letter had been waiting for them in New York, a jubilant, foolish letter, signed by three foolish old people. "We've got a producer," they wrote, "the show's going on!" Grant did not really want to see his father.

She took two days and went alone to see her own father. Everything was the same. The house was so quiet and he so still that two days were too long. She flew back to Grant.

"Sure you're quite well?" she asked, leaning from the train to kiss her father.

"Yes, of course," he said. He smiled dimly. "My life's over, you know. I'm just waiting."

On the train she pondered why it was that there can never be equals in marriage. One always draws from the other. Since her flashing little mother died, her father had been only a shadow. While she lived he had had substance and meaning, but when she went, she had taken with her his substance, too.

The school year began again and she went faithfully and against her will back and forth to her classes. She had stopped thinking about ghosts. Indeed, she had forgotten them. This was now her normal life. She was head of the committee this year for the faculty reception to the new students. Mrs. Benton was busy heading up a drive for a million-dollar endowment. At the very last moment of vacation Mrs. Petrie had decided to stay on in Paris. Mrs. Benton drove everybody harder because of it. The million-dollar endowment, which had for years been only a pleasant dream for which everybody worked, now became a necessity for Mrs. Benton to accomplish. She hired a professional fund raiser with whom she sat in long hours of conferences, and she began to look at Elinor.

"I know Mrs. Benton is going to ask me to do something," she told Grant. "I can tell by the way she looks at me."

Almost at once Mrs. Benton came to see them. It was evening. They were both correcting themes now, pausing sometimes to read bits aloud or to discuss together some rule of style or fact.

"Damn," Grant said softly when the doorbell rang.

"I'll go," she said. It occurred to her as she put down her pen that Grant demurred rather less than he used to do when she offered to go to the door. His "Let me, darling" was not so quick as it had been. It was not worth thinking about. She opened the door on Mrs. Benton.

"Come in," she said.

"I just had a little matter of business," Mrs. Benton began.

"Come into the living room," Elinor said. Behind Mrs. Benton and over her head she made a little face at Grant and shaped her lips into "I told you so!"

"It just occurred to me," said Mrs. Benton, sitting down and smiling painstakingly at Grant, "that your wife is the youngest and prettiest woman on the faculty."

"No!" Grant exclaimed, twinkling.

"And," Mrs. Benton went on, "she'd therefore be the very one to do some speaking for the endowment."

"Oh no!" Elinor exclaimed. "I couldn't—I never have—"

"I'm sure you could," Mrs. Benton said. "I've always noticed that when you have a report or something on a committee, you do it so well—" She turned to Grant. "She thinks on her feet, Professor, and that's so rare."

"Yes, it is," Grant said.

"Grant, I couldn't!" Elinor repeated. "Please!"

She turned to him, sure that he would reinforce her. She didn't want to have to leave home and go out and make speeches. But she was astonished to see pleasure in Grant's look and his smile approved not her, but Mrs. Benton.

"I don't know, Elinor," he said warmly, "I don't see why you can't. You've always been able to do things."

She felt he was siding with the enemy against her. She wanted to say firmly and at once, "I won't do it, Grant." But she did not. She sat silent, compelled by his approval.

"You could begin just with the Rotarians here in our own town," Mrs. Benton said. She opened her bag and hunted for a letter. "Here their letter is. I brought it just in case. They say, 'We will be very glad to turn our October meeting over to you and your associates in this worthy cause.' That would be just the meeting for you, my dear."

Elinor turned helplessly to Grant. But he did not look at her. "I don't see why not," he was saying. "I don't at all see why not."

The strangest thing of all was that once she began she liked it. For days before the meeting she had gone half sick with dread and every time she thought of the moment to come her tongue went dry in her mouth. But when the actual moment came after luncheon and she rose amidst hand-clapping and looked upon the room full of listening faces, her fear left her and a certain power came into her. She began to speak easily and fearlessly, her low voice pitched clearly into the middle of the room, and a new conviction carried her along. She began to feel as she talked that Mrs. Benton was right. They needed the million dollars and they needed it now. Her voice took on added earnestness and her thoughts shaped themselves convincingly. She put down the notes she had made. She really could think on her feet.

Afterward they crowded around her and shook her hand. She heard one after another say, "I guess you're right, little lady." "I guess we ought to do something for the old alma mater—" "Might as well do it now—we'll never be richer with things going on as they are." She listened, smiling and full of a sort of pleasure nothing had ever given her before. She felt powerful and intelligent and useful. Grant was waiting with her coat and his face was shining with pride. "You did beautifully," he whispered. "I was so proud I could scarcely keep from shouting to everybody, 'She's my wife!' " There had not been a look like that in his face before, no, not for anything— not even the day he told her he loved her.

When Mrs. Benton came to suggest, "Now that our own Rotary has responded so wonderfully, dear, do you think you'd mind going over to Clintonville? They're so anxious to have you. I guess your fame has gone abroad," she felt no pain at all. Besides, Grant was saying, "Why not? It's a good cause."

That was the beginning of her winter tour. She covered three states and the faculty appointed young Mr.

Brady, the third assistant in the English department, to take her classes when she was gone. By February the million-dollar endowment was well under way. Mrs. Petrie was home from Paris by Christmas, looking more beautiful than ever. "Oh dear," she cried to Elinor, "what's all this about your being a wonderful speaker and organizer? I must come the very next time." She put down upon a bit of paper the day and hour of Elinor's address to the Tuesday Morning Club, but when Elinor rose to speak, Mrs. Petrie was not there.

Three days later Mrs. Benton exclaimed before her, "You should have heard our Elinor on Tuesday—she was marvelous."

"What?" said Mrs. Petrie. She had come in very late to a faculty party. "Oh, I say, Elinor, my dear, I forgot!"

"It doesn't matter," Elinor said. She spoke honestly, hating herself for minding it.

"Oh well," Mrs. Petrie said contentedly, "nobody cares what I do—they know it doesn't matter."

"As if that excused her!" Mrs. Benton whispered with anger. But Mrs. Petrie was talking to someone else. She had forgotten again.

It was really exciting to discover in herself this new gift. She no longer dreaded any crowd. She knew that as soon as she rose to her feet, her material organized and stored in her mind, that reassuring strength would mount and take possession of her. And in a moment she would hear her voice begin, calm and strong, and faces would turn to her and movement be arrested, and that subtle stream of accord between her and her audience would begin to flow.

Dr. Petrie came to see her one day. She and Grant were about to go out for golf—they had taken it up recently as her speaking brought them new friends.

"I won't keep you," Dr. Petrie said. He stood in the hall, tall and always a little diffident. It was hard to believe sometimes that he was the important person he was in education and economics, the author of standard books and a successful college president.

"Come in, come in," Grant said heartily. Everybody liked Dr. Petrie. They put down their golf things and went into the living room and Dr. Petrie began at once, his shy smile lighting all he said.

"I have come to ask a great favor, Mrs. Seabury. We've been so impressed with the work you have been doing on the endowment fund. Dean Benton feels that we owe more to you than to anyone else. It's been extraordinary."

His warm, kind eyes praised her and Grant said impulsively, "Isn't it splendid?"

"Yes, it is," Dr. Petrie agreed. "And now, will you do more for us? It seems ingratitude, doesn't it! But will you make a little tour for us to all the alumni centers and tell them just what you've been telling the people here?"

She looked at Grant.

"Why not?" he said eagerly.

"No, but—I'd have to—how long would I have to be away from home?" she faltered.

"Well, not more than a month, or perhaps six weeks," said Dr. Petrie. "It would be a great help."

She looked at Grant again.

"You'd be alone," she said.

"I'll manage," said Grant, "for such a good cause."

"Thank you, Seabury," said Dr. Petrie, "thank you very much. Now I won't keep you from your game."

"When must I start?" Elinor asked.

"Next week?" Dr. Petrie suggested.

She spent the last few days teaching Dillie everything about Grant's likes and needs. She wrote down on sheets of paper, one for every day of the week, exactly what Grant must have to eat. Once she caught herself. "Broiled chops and peas—" She paused, her pencil at her lips. There was a ghostly familiarity about that. Then she went on briskly. It was silly to think about ghosts. Besides, if she didn't write down menus, Dillie would serve nothing but hamburger and cauliflower. Her imagination ran no further.

There was one moment on the train, at the very last, when she wished she were not going. "Oh, Grant," she cried, her face in his coat, "I don't think I like this!"

"Cheer up, darling," he said, patting her. "You're going to be the biggest sort of success. I'm terribly proud of you."

She lifted her head at that and smiled at him. And when the whistle blew and he had to get off, she waved to him through the window. She was going to be a success. And when the train had pulled away and she could not see him anymore, she thought of how proud he would be of her when she came back.

At every hotel during that month she seized Grant's letters and read them first, before she did anything. He was getting on very well—missing her, but so proud of her. Dillie was doing exactly as she had been told. Everything was clockwork. She mustn't worry—just throw herself into her job. When she came home he wanted to talk over with her the matter of really going on the lecture platform, now that she had shown this gift. But he'd wait. And now, a little advice about reporters. He'd had experience at that with Mother. She went back to the first page.

He was so proud of her.

"You see, sweet, I've had a lot of time to think while you were away." It was their first moment alone since she had come home. She had been met at the train by a delegation and they had gone straight to Dean Benton's house for tea and everybody wanted to hear about her trip. Mrs. Benton was bustling everywhere, pushing the small, quiet dean here and there. He was trying to help with the cups, but she said plainly, "Just sit down, please, Jonathan. It isn't necessary."

And when the moment came it was Mrs. Benton who rose and said, "Now if everybody will come to order, please!" She clapped her hands and silence fell. She began again. "We are all so excited over the news that all the endowment is pledged and our dear Mrs. Seabury has been the one—"

Elinor shrank a little. Dr. Petrie, sitting beside her, was looking quietly out the window, not listening. Mrs. Petrie had not come, but then, no one expected her.

"Now, Mrs. Seabury!" Mrs. Benton was commanding her. "Come to the front, please."

She shook her head and rose, clinging to the chair ahead of her. "I'll just stay here, if you don't mind," she said. "There isn't much to tell."

At the sound of her voice Dr. Petrie's head turned toward her attentively.

After it was all over she and Grant were alone. Ah, but it was good to get into her old blue velvet housecoat and slippers and patter downstairs to the fire beside him.

"I'm a home woman," she had whispered into his shoulder.

"Like hell you are," he had said, laughing. "Say, sweet—" and then he had gone on to tell her what it was he had been thinking about.

"Why shouldn't we develop you?" he demanded. "You've got a career ahead of you, Elinor. Everybody says so. It's extraordinary, and we must make the most of it. Now that this job's done, you could branch out into something else—politics, maybe, or some phase of national life connected with women, you know. That's where the money is—lecturing for women. Not that I want you to do it for money, you know. But it would be a public education."

"Public education?" she murmured, inquiring. "I don't want to—"

But he did not hear her. He was filling his pipe quickly, excited by his own plans.

"You might make a book out of your lectures," he said. "Mother was always going to do that and would have—if she'd lived. Now we'll prepare for that by writing each lecture fully—hire a stenographer to take it all down. It's never so spontaneous if you try to write it down afterward. Say, darling, you need a manager, and I'll be the chap."

"But your own work—" she faltered. She was sitting upright now, not leaning on him anymore. She didn't know what to think—she wasn't sure—

"Oh, I'll do that, too," he said carelessly. "There's more future in you than in a bunch of students. Oh, you darling!"

He swept her in his arms passionately and she could not refuse his adoration. No, it was lovely to be adored and worshiped. She did not say a word when after their dinner he brought out a folder of clippings and began eagerly.

"I've kept a file of possible causes, Elinor. I wouldn't want you to take up anything just because I say so. You must really feel it yourself, or you can't make a success of it."

She took each bit of paper as he handed it to her. "Are Women as Creative as Men?" she read. "Women versus Men in Politics." "League for Political Education of Women Holds Meeting—"

She put them all down. "I think I won't decide to-night, Grant," she said. "I've only just come home."

He swept them all back into the folder. "No, of course not," he said tenderly. "You're tired." He laid the folder on the table, and went to the radio and searched the air until he found a quiet bit of chamber music. Then he drew her to the couch beside him.

"Rest," he whispered, "rest."

She put her head on his breast and closed her eyes and lay very still. But under her cheek she could feel the furious pounding of his heart. The blood was racing back and forth to supply his busy, planning brain. He turned and kissed her hard once. "There's just one more thing," he said. "I'm not going to urge you, Elinor. But when you have decided, will you tell me?"

"Yes," she promised.

The music was quiet as a night sky, but his heart was pounding on.

She could not make up her mind. Alone in the house sometimes, she thought, I want to stay at home. I don't want to do anything else. The house was dear and still around her. She loved caring for it and planning for it.

And yet it was also pleasant to have everyone admiring and warm. Dr. Petrie came to consult her twice on the endowment fund. Even in her class the students were nearly deferential.

"Gosh, Mrs. Seabury," a tall lad murmured, "we think it was swell—what you did, you know."

"It was thrilling," an eager girl chimed in. "I wonder if you know what an inspiration you are to us. It's so excit-ing to see a woman who doesn't just sit, and whose brains aren't simply drugged by bridge!"

Alone, she searched herself. Grant said, "You must feel your cause, of course." What did she feel? That was the exciting thing. She really could feel several things. If she let herself, she could believe that women ought to run more for public office, for instance. It was shameful the way women settled for the security of home and allowed their minds to degenerate. Almost no women had any real interests beyond amusement. Her own mother, for instance—she had been dear and amusing, but after all—

And then suddenly one day Mr. Seabury came to see them. He had grown so dilatory about writing to them that once or twice she had been a little worried about him.

"Grant, your father hasn't written for *weeks!*"

"Oh, well," Grant had said, "if anything were wrong, we'd hear."

They had not heard. So she was quite unprepared for him when she opened the door and found him there. A cabman was bringing his bag from a taxi at the curb.

"Well, Elinor," he said mildly.

"Why, Mr. Seabury!" she cried.

"I thought I'd come to see you," he said.

"Yes, of course. Do come in," she stammered. "Did you send us a letter or something? I mean, is it our fault we didn't know you were coming?"

"No," he said, "no."

He tipped the cabman lavishly and came in. He was looking so spruce and gay she did not know him. "The fact is," he said, taking off a bright plaid scarf and a new tweed topcoat, "I didn't write because I didn't know what to say. We've been busy on the play—"

"Aren't you working at the bank anymore?"

"No," he said gently, "no. I quit that a good while ago, but I told your dad I'd just as soon he didn't say anything. The play takes a good deal of time."

She took him into the living room.

"How is the play?" she inquired.

He sat down and lit a cigar. Mr. Seabury and a cigar! Grant's mother had hated cigars.

"It's ready," he said in a solemn voice. "It's going to open day after tomorrow. I came to tell you and see if you and Grant could come up for it. You're to have the best seats in the house."

"Who's producing it?" she asked.

"We are," he said. "Peter and Mrs. Cassels and I. You know, Peter's got real dramatic sense. I don't think Ethel ever understood him. And Mrs. Cassels—" He paused and flicked the ash from his cigar. "Well, I guess I didn't know there were any women like her." He paused again and went on. His low, slightly melancholy voice was all that seemed left of Mr. Seabury. Surely his hair was darker than she remembered it? At least, he had never worn a signet ring before, nor a fancy waistcoat. "Ethel," he began, "was a noble woman—" He looked up at her secretively, and a slow, impish smile began to come up in his eyes. "She was damned noble," he said gently, "and I've had enough of it for a lifetime."

She laughed. "Don't let Grant hear you," she said.

"No," he whispered. "I never have. Well"—his voice grew natural—"what about the show?"

"We'll come," she said gaily. Her heart lifted. There was something about Mr. Seabury that made her feel careless and full of mischief. Grant would be disgusted with him. Grant wouldn't want to go to the show, maybe.

"Of course, we'll come," she promised.

"That's fine," he said. "And now, if you're not busy, let's see the town."

She spent the afternoon with Mr. Seabury. He stood

beside her looking reflectively at the ivy-covered chapel, and in the library he coughed, carefully silent.

"Hm," he said, "it all looks very familiar."

They walked home together in the cold early twilight.

"Do you think the play will be a success?" she asked. "Oh, I hope so."

"I don't know," Mr. Seabury said. "Sometimes I think it isn't such a good play, maybe. But it doesn't matter about success—I've had what I wanted out of it already. It's making a play work that's such fun." He paused a moment. "I suppose Grant won't see that," he said slowly. "If it isn't a success I suppose Grant will say it is what he expected."

"Oh no," Elinor said, "you mustn't feel that about him. He isn't really like that."

"I don't know what he is," Mr. Seabury said.

They were going up the steps and she saw a light in Grant's study.

"Excuse me," she said, "I'll just tell Grant—" She hurried ahead of him and ran into Grant's study. He was at his desk. "Your dad's here," she sang aloud. Then she bent over him and whispered fiercely, "Their play's going to open day after tomorrow and we must go to the opening. Grant, promise me you'll go!"

He looked up. "Why, if you care—" he said.

"I do—I do—" she whispered, and did not know why she did, except that none of them must be hurt, Mr. Seabury and Peter and Mrs. Cassels. Nobody like them must be hurt. Why should she think at that moment of Dean Benton's quiet, withered face? And of Mrs. Petrie?

"Be kind, Grant!" she begged him.

He rose and put his arm around her shoulder.

"Why, Elinor," he said, surprised. "I am always kind, I think."

"No, but *feel* kind to him," she begged.

"Hello, Grant!" his father said from the door. He was looking at his son shyly.

"I've just been telling Grant about the play," Elinor said fervently. "He thinks it's wonderful, don't you, Grant?" She pressed Grant's arm and felt the muscles grow tense in her fingers.

"I'm sure it is," Grant's polite voice said. She pressed his arm harder. "Of course it is," he repeated more loudly.

"Well," said Mr. Seabury, "I wasn't sure how you'd take it." He straightened himself and smiled with the angelic relief of a child who is, after all, not going to be scolded. Then he took out a cigar.

"Have one," he said to Grant.

Mrs. Petrie had never come to see her before. She never really went to see anybody. In spring she might pass the garden gate and stop and walk about the flower-beds to see what was coming up. She loved flowers. But if you said, "Won't you come in, Mrs. Petrie?" she always shook her hatless head and said, "Oh no, not today, thanks. I'm just on my way." Her great, quick smile would glow around the words and make them gentle.

"Some other time, then?"

"Sometime." And she would open the gate and walk away with her swift and swinging step.

But this morning she passed straight by the budding crocuses and came up the steps and rang the doorbell. Through the window Elinor saw her and she went and opened the door. It was somehow exciting to see Mrs. Petrie standing there, big and glowing with exercise.

"Good morning!" Her round deep voice rolled out like

a bell. "Are you alone, and if you are, may I come in?"

"I am, and you may," Elinor said.

It was the morning of the play. Grant had taken his father to the station early and then he had gone to class. She was sitting at his desk, looking over the clippings he had filed for her neatly, and making up her mind. At the moment when the doorbell rang she had been wondering why she had not wanted to tell Mr. Seabury anything about their plans. When Grant had begun, once, "What do you think our Elinor is going to do?" she cried out, "Oh, Grant, don't say anything now!"

"Come into the living room," she said to Mrs. Petrie.

Mrs. Petrie came in and sat down and unbuttoned her short dark green jacket and drew off her old brown gloves.

"I was just walking past," she said in her rushing voice, "and I was thinking of you, and so I decided to come in and tell you what I was thinking."

"I'm glad," Elinor murmured. She was a little dazed by Mrs. Petrie's big, warm, brown eyes, fixed ardently upon her. Why should Mrs. Petrie be thinking of her?

"Everybody admires you so much," Mrs. Petrie said, "and so do I." She smiled and Elinor felt warm light wrapping her about. "But it's not just that—it's that there's something in you that makes me think of myself—once—and I wanted to tell you about that."

"I'm glad," Elinor said again. She had no idea what Mrs. Petrie meant.

"That's a lovely thing," Mrs. Petrie said suddenly. She leaned forward and touched a pot of early tulips. She glowed at it a moment, seeming to forget what she had said. "Did you buy them or raise them?"

"I raised them," Elinor said.

"They look as though they'd grown quietly at home,"

Mrs. Petrie said, "where they had time to make long roots. The petals are so strong and full of color. The bought ones, I think, always look hurried and sort of on show." She felt the texture of a petal. "Yes," she murmured, "like good satin instead of gold tissue."

Elinor gazed at her. There was much of the born actress about this woman, the unconscious great actress, feeling drama in every second of life. She felt as though she were sitting alone in a theater, watching.

"Are you going on with this lecturing?" Mrs. Petrie asked abruptly.

"I don't—my husband wants me to do it," she answered, surprised.

"You don't care much about it, I think," Mrs. Petrie said. It might have been casually said except that nothing such a voice could say was casual. And then Mrs. Petrie looked at her again, closely, demanding the truth.

"When I'm not doing it, I don't," Elinor said, and waited a moment, hunting for the truth. "But when I do it, it seems exciting." She searched out the last bit of truth. "Grant likes me to do it," she repeated. She felt somehow she must defend herself against Mrs. Petrie.

Mrs. Petrie was touching a tulip leaf again.

"Do you know, we'd hoped—my husband and I—to see Grant made full professor next autumn." Elinor's breath jumped. That meant— But Mrs. Petrie's voice was going on. "But somehow he doesn't seem to care enough about himself. He does his work, of course, conscientiously, but there's no flair." She stopped a second and went on. "It's almost as though he were more interested in something else."

She did not answer. She sat very still, waiting.

"Will you tell me exactly what you mean, Mrs. Petrie?" she asked at last.

"Yes, I will," Mrs. Petrie said. She turned herself warmly toward Elinor. "My dear, you're at a place where so many women stand nowadays. I stood there once. You know I was in opera? Yes, well, I was, and it didn't occur to me to give it up. And Dan wouldn't hear of it." Mrs. Petrie smiled, remembering, caressing the tulip. "So I didn't give it up. I came and went in my footloose fashion, and everything worked very well— there weren't any children, you see. And then, suddenly, I discovered that Dan was thinking of giving up his job."

"Dr. Petrie?" Elinor's voice was unbelieving. She could not imagine Dr. Petrie without his quiet tenacity of devotion to his job. Mrs. Petrie nodded.

"Yes, he nearly did. We were happy—it wasn't that— it wasn't that I was away—I've always come and gone, willful woman that I am. It was something else."

"Yes?" Elinor said steadily. She must see clearly what Mrs. Petrie wanted her to see.

"We had to have the same center, do you see? When two people are close, there can't be two centers. It's like whirling concentric circles—they've got to whirl around the same center if they're to stay together, because if they whirl about two centers they tend to draw away from each other." She paused again and spread a tulip's petals wide and stared down into its yellow calyx. Then she let the petals spring back and looked up. "If two people love each other very much—so they can't draw away—then one of them holds the center, don't you think? And the other one is drawn into it—as though it were a whirlpool." She put the tulips aside. "Well, Dan was being drawn into my whirlpool. And I knew he'd be lost. Besides, I didn't want him to be like that. So I gave it up." She laughed. "Minnie Benton never understood that—poor Jonathan Benton! He's sweet, if he is henpecked—you know, everybody thought he'd be chosen president instead of Dan, but the trustees said they couldn't be sure Minnie wouldn't—well, that's old gossip. Jonathan's been lovely to us. No one could ever guess that Dan's taken his dream away."

Elinor was sitting very still. Lately, it was true, Grant had said little about his own work. He had been busy planning for her.

Mrs. Petrie rose abruptly, unfolding her long legs. She was very tall, and a little loose-jointed. "Well, that's all. I can't talk much—never could. But Grant's quite a brilliant chap, Dan says. Perhaps you are brilliant, too. I don't know. Anyway, those circles—" She was twisting an orange scarf about her neck. "You know, just after you were married, Grant was wonderful, Dan said. Before, he had been promising, but there was a sort of shadow over him—and somehow it's back again." She felt among the tulips with big delicate fingers. "Do you mind if I take just this gold one?"

"No, take it," Elinor said. She wanted to say, "Thank you, Mrs. Petrie," but she was not sure what Mrs. Petrie had said.

Mrs. Petrie, her hand on the door, was smiling down at her. "I'm not good at talking," she said, "I've always sung."

She was gone. The room was full of haunting echoes of the deep and lovely voice, and Elinor stood among them, listening, catching them to remember the words that they had carried.

I know what she means, she thought fervently, because I know what she is.

The play was a complete failure. How, she wondered in amazement, could those three people ever have seen anything in this sentimental, foolish play about an old man on a park bench dreaming his life over again? All the old themes were there, home and mother, the wrong woman, the frustrated dream of music—and then the life as it might have been—the right woman, love, success—and the old man dead on the park bench, smiling happily. She was sitting between Peter and Mrs. Cassels.

"Oh dear, I always cry," Mrs. Cassels said happily. "It's so sweet, isn't it?"

"Great box office stuff," Peter was whispering huskily.

Beyond, she saw Grant's stern, strained profile. And beyond that Mr. Seabury, wistful, smiling, his lips parted.

It was perfectly evident what people thought. They laughed and laughed. In a few hours newspapers would carry the wet ink of critics. "A new revelation of tripe—" "To what depths bosh will sink—"

But these three people were gazing at the stage, living again. Even Peter, smelling strongly of rye whiskey, his red hands on his knees, was gazing soberly, his eyes misted, at the old man on the park bench whose hand was drooping on his breast. The curtain fell, and they went in silence through the crowd. She took Grant's hand and squeezed it.

"They had a good time, remember," she whispered. "Nothing else matters, really."

"Goodbye, goodbye," she said to them at the curb. "It was touching and I'm glad we came."

"Goodbye," Grant said grimly. "Good luck."

They watched the three of them go down the street, Mrs. Cassels trotting a little, a hand in each arm beside her.

"Fools!" Grant muttered passionately. "I'm glad Mother wasn't here to see it! What they'll live on now, I don't know. They've spent everything."

"Mrs. Cassels has her alimony," Elinor suggested.

"And thank God, Mother knew my father well enough not to trust him," Grant said bitterly. "People like that simply have to be taken care of by somebody. Well, Peter can beg from them."

They hurried to the train and barely caught it. The play did not matter. All day, since Mrs. Petrie had come, nothing else was important. They settled themselves in a nearly empty car.

"When I think of my mother," Grant was saying passionately, "I thank God I married you, Elinor. I thank God you're no fool. Sometimes I think everybody is more or less of a fool in one way or another. Only you are not. When I look at other people I say to myself, thank God I found a wonderful woman and married her."

A wonderful woman! She felt as though she had been pierced with a javelin thrown from afar. Surely Grant had not thrown it. No, he had not meant it. But she saw herself—why, she was Mrs. Seabury. Grant had been making her into his mother, shaping her, urging her into his mother. Ever since the biography was finished he had been doing it. And she had been helpless in his hands because she loved him. She never quite forgot that she had loved Grant before he loved her. And so she had been too anxious to keep him pleased.

"I won't be—her," she muttered under her breath.

"What's that?" he asked.

She crumpled against Grant childishly. "Don't," she whispered. She pressed her face into his coat.

"What's the matter?" he asked, amazed.

"I don't want to make any more speeches," she murmured. "I hate doing it—"

His arm stiffened a little around her. "You mean—then why didn't you tell me?" he demanded.

"I thought I had to, because you wanted me to be like that," she said.

"I do want you to—use your gifts," he said gravely.

She shook her head. "I don't want to," she said. It wasn't her gift—it was Mrs. Seabury's.

He drew away from her a little. "Do you mean, Elinor, that you want to give up all our plans?"

She nodded. He stared at her. He was displeased, but it didn't matter. Even though he were angry with her for a while, it was better for him. Now she knew exactly why Mrs. Petrie had come to see her. Grant must be free of the shadow of his mother, even though he made the shadow for himself and wanted it and loved it. He must be driven out into the light, where he could be himself.

"You've been making a wonderful woman of me," she said. "You've been wanting something I'm not."

Ghosts, that was what. He wanted a ghost.

"I'm an ordinary, living woman," she said, "nothing wonderful. I hate wonderful women. It frightens me to think I'd have to be one. Don't make me, darling!"

She curled against him. But he was still stiff.

"Certainly I don't want you to be anything you don't want to be and aren't."

The train swerved around a curve and pushed them together.

"Do you mean you don't want to do anything about the political league for women and all that?" he asked.

"Nothing," she said.

"What do you want, then?" he demanded.

"Just to be your wife," she said.

But he was not pleased.

"It's medieval," he said after a moment.

"Yes, it is," she agreed.

He stared at her. "Haven't you any ambition?"

"Lots," she said, "for you."

Off in the dark night sky she could see two flaming, whirling circles coming close together.

"They're just waiting to make you a full professor," she said.

"No!" Grant cried. "How do you know?" He drew away to look at her excitedly.

"Mrs. Petrie told me this morning."

Grant squeezed her in his arms. "I wouldn't have said so for anything, Elinor, but now I'll tell you I've been a little hurt that it hasn't happened. Why didn't you tell me before?"

"Books," she murmured. "I want you to write books. I want you to be famous."

The two circles were very near, now.

"Suppose," she whispered, "suppose you should ever dream and wish your life were different? Like that old man?"

"Rotten play," Grant said.

"Yes, but those three—they were the old man—that's why they loved it."

"Oh, well—those three—"

"Silly, aren't they," she agreed. "Still—"

They were silent a moment. Then Grant spoke, his voice amazingly shy. "Did Mrs. Petrie say when?"

"Soon, I think—very soon. As soon as something was passed."

"A vote, I suppose."

She nodded. No, a shadow, she thought, but she said nothing.

"Well," said Grant, pulling down his hat, "I shall have to apply myself." He had forgotten all about her, she perceived happily. Tomorrow she would go over to see Mrs. Petrie. She was going to be very good friends with

Mrs. Petrie. Mrs. Benton—well, Mrs. Benton would have to bear it.

"I think I'll begin that research I've always wanted to do." Grant was frowning. "You know—the influence of Oriental philosophy on early American writers—the tea traders and all that—"

"Why not?" Elinor said.

The train was coming to a stop. They were back. Their car stood where they had left it. They stepped into it and in a few minutes they were home again. She stood inside the door a second, feeling. There were no ghosts—not one.

"*You're* wonderful, you know," she said to Grant. "*You* can do anything. Besides, one in a family's enough."

"Kiss me," he said.

She gave herself up to him triumphantly, her eyes wide open. She was doing exactly what she wanted to do. And how she was going to make Grant work! There were going to be no more wonderful women for him—no, no, only she, clinging around his neck, urging him on, depending on him, forcing him by her pride and her praise to be busy and famous. He reached for her and crushed her in his arms, coat and all. There was a faint click, as though somewhere in space a circle sprang concentric to another's axis. Then they went whirling on as one. She smiled suddenly, secretly, over Grant's shoulder. What a good time she and Mrs. Petrie were going to have!

Here and Now

"I SHALL SAY GOODBYE only seven more times, Julia."

Julia Barry looked up into the dark eyes just above her own and smiled.

"Only seven more times," she agreed. She put up her hand and with her forefinger she followed the fine line of Rodney's eyebrow.

She felt his arms tighten around her. "You wouldn't think it possible to make it Monday instead of Thursday?"

"I couldn't make it possible," she said and laughed.

"Why not," he pleaded, "since it's not a wedding?"

"It's our marriage," she said, "and I won't have it shifted around anyhow. Thursday I said and Thursday it is. All my thinking about it is Thursday."

"Do you think about it?" he whispered.

"Night and day," she said.

"So do I," he said gravely, "night and day. No doubts?"

"None," she said.

His arms loosened a little, but she knew he did not know it. His handsome face was grave, and the gravity suited his silver-gray hair. "I don't want you to have any doubts—because of what happened before."

"I don't think of that," she said. "That's finished and gone. This is my real marriage."

93

"That's what I feel," he said. "Mary died so young." Mary had been his first wife.

They kissed each other with intense love, two middle-aged people, and then he went away and she stood in the door and watched his tall, straight figure until she could see it no more in the dimness of the street lights.

It was a spring night, and it was late, long after midnight. But she felt too restless to go to bed, and so she went out the open french window of the living room to the terrace and stretched herself in a long chair. The moonlight poured down on her and she felt bathed in it. It was cool and magnetic—she could imagine that the rays tingled in her body. She would lie here until Meira came in from her dance.

But even as she decided this the side gate of the garden opened and she saw Meira and Robert. They stood a moment in the shadows and then she saw her young daughter turn and fling herself into the arms of the man. She did not move, but the sight shook her to the heart. Meira, at eighteen! It was too young. Then she remembered that she, too, had been only eighteen when she had fallen in love with Harry Trainor—with Harry, who was Meira's father. Yes, but what marriage it had been, ending so quickly that Meira could not remember when she had lived in the house with both of them! They had parted hating each other so passionately that she smiled sadly, remembering both love and hate. No wonder that love had burned so quickly away—no one could have endured it.

"Meira!" she called sharply.

The two figures parted reluctantly but without shame and then came toward her in the moonlight, hand in hand, and laughing.

"We didn't see you, Mother," Meira said cheerfully.

"I hope you don't mind, Mrs. Barry," Robert said.

"But I do mind," she said. To her own surprise she felt a strange, jealous severity. But she made her voice light. "It's disturbing to see my only child so suddenly— enveloped."

"Sorry," the young man said imperturbably. He put his arm around Meira and drew her close to him. She was so small that she seemed to melt into a slender white line against his black evening clothes. "But you'll have to get used to it, I'm afraid, Mrs. Barry."

"We're going to be married, Mother," Meira said. She had a high, clear, little voice that remained childish in all its tones.

"Oh, Meira," Julia cried.

"Yes, Mother," Meira said. "You're not the only one. You can't just decide to get married and leave me—"

"Darling, you aren't being left—we're going to live here as we always have. And you know I came and asked you if you'd mind Rodney—"

Meira laughed and pulled herself free and flung herself beside her mother, a froth of white organdy ruffles and yellow curls. "I'm only teasing," she said joyously. "I think it's wonderful for you and Rodney to get married. We think everybody ought to get married, don't we, Rob?"

The young man dropped on the terrace steps, admiring the two women in the moonlight. He was a painter on weekends and holidays, whenever his father let him off from the business, and he could admire the contrast between the blond young girl and the beautiful dark-haired woman who was her mother. Meira's father was blond, Meira had told him, and she looked like him.

"I think *we* ought to get married," he said laughing, "and certainly I don't blame anybody for wanting to marry you, Mrs. Barry. Gee, you look swell in the moonlight!"

"But at eighteen, Meira, and Rob, you're only twenty-one!"

"Why wait, if we know what we want?" Meira's young voice cut across her mother's like a silver knife.

"But you can't know—darling. I thought I knew—at eighteen—and I didn't know until I was thirty-five and met Rodney—and now it's taken me two years to be sure. I'm getting really married only at thirty-seven."

"If you hadn't made your mistake at eighteen," Meira said, "I wouldn't have been born." She turned her golden head. "Rob, what if I hadn't been born?"

"It wasn't a mistake, Mrs. Barry," he said gravely, "not if it meant Meira."

Julia did not answer. She could not, indeed. These children had answered for themselves. Whatever gave them life—could it be a mistake?

"But I mean—as a marriage—" she said indistinctly, "We were so unhappy—there was so much quarreling."

"What about?" Meira asked.

"Oh, I don't remember," she said unwillingly. "I remember only the bitterness—and how we parted."

Meira leaned forward. "Mother, have you ever been sorry you and he—left each other?"

"No," Julia said quickly, "never—never!"

She looked from one solemn young face to the other and then she put out her hand and touched her daughter's cheek. "Yes, you were the one good thing that came out of that poor, silly, young marriage."

Silence followed her words. The two children looked away from each other. Meira dropped her head and smoothed out a ruffle, and Robert stooped and picked up a pebble from the gravel of the garden walk and tossed it as far as he could. Then he rose and straightened his shoulders.

"It's getting late," he said. "I guess I'd better be going, Meira. See you tomorrow?"

"Maybe," she said. "I don't know."

He hesitated a moment. "Will you call up or shall I?"

She shook her head. "I—don't know."

"Then I'll call you," he said. "Goodnight."

"Night," Meira said.

"What's the matter with you two?" Julia asked, in surprise.

But Rob was already walking down the path and now he was at the gate.

"Nothing," Meira said. She rose and bent to kiss her mother's cheek. "Goodnight, Mother," and she was gone, like a cloud.

The garden air was suddenly chilly with night. Julia rose after a moment and went inside and closed the windows behind her and went upstairs.

"I hurt them," she thought. "In some foolish fashion I hurt their feelings."

She lay awake a while wondering what she had done. Children, she thought, they're so tender and new, like butterflies. One hurts them without knowing it and then they don't fly.

It was the strangest thing in the world to see lying at her place the next morning a letter from Harry. She did not think of Harry from year's end to year's end, and then last night she had thought of him a good deal because of Rob and Meira. And as if he had known it, he had written this letter. No, that was ridiculous, because of course the letter was already written and mailed two days ago.

She let it lie a long moment while she took up the violets that Rodney had sent. He sent her flowers every morning but violets were her favorite. Next week when she was married she would carry violets, a great bunch of them with her gray satin dress. She lifted them now to her face and felt them soft against her cheek. She closed her eyes for a moment, being alone. I love you, Rodney, she thought. Yes, she loved him as she had not known how to love that passionate, spoiled blond boy years ago. This was love, whatever that had been.

Then she took up Harry's letter. It was brief enough, and his handwriting had not changed. It was still the boyish scrawl she used to find inside bouquets and books and boxes of candy. But there was no lovemaking in it. She read it quickly.

"Dear Julia, I happen to be going through the old town on Friday on business, and I'd like to see you for old times' sake. I take it that we have got over past grudges. Maybe you don't want to see me, and if you don't, it's all right. But I'd like to hear about Meira. She must be a big girl. I'll wait for you at Timmie's Place. If you don't show up by half past one, I'll go on. Harry."

Timmie's Place was where they had been used to meeting in those years when they were children. She had not gone there once since the days she had gone with him. No one would know her there, now.

She tore the letter up very fine and left the bits in a small heap under the other envelopes. Why should she meet Harry? What had they to say to each other now? There was Meira, of course. She sat for a long time, sipping her coffee, and looking thoughtfully at the violets on the table before her. Then she rose and went to the telephone and called Rodney, as she did every morning.

But this morning it was a little different. Should she tell him that she had had a letter from Harry? Should she tell him she was not going?

"Julia?" His voice, very deep and calm, was at her ear.

"Yes," she said.

"I was waiting for you to call before I went to a meeting at the other end of town—I can't go off without your voice fresh in me every morning."

"My day doesn't begin until I call you, Rodney."

"I wish I could have luncheon with you today."

"I wish you could." Suddenly she knew she had to tell him. "Rodney?"

"Yes, my dearest?"

"I had a letter from Harry today—the first in all these years."

There was a pause and it grew so long she called, "Rodney, are you there?"

His voice came back instantly. "Yes, certainly I am here. I was just thinking—wondering—"

"He happens to be passing through town today and wants me to have lunch with him."

"Do you want to have lunch with him, Julia?"

"I don't think so."

"Then why do it?"

"I wouldn't, only—"

"Only what, Julia?"

"Rodney, Rob and Meira are engaged—they're so young—"

"What's that got to do with—"

"Only that somehow I keep thinking about Harry and me—so young—it was such a mistake—and yet dare I tell Meira she mustn't?"

"Are you going to talk about that with Harry?"

"Dearest, I thought I wasn't to go—"

"I think you'd better go—I think you want to go, Julia."

"Rodney, no—it's only that if I see him I feel I might be able better to know what to do about Meira."

"Are you making an excuse of Meira?"

She gasped at the pain in his voice, "Rodney, are you angry?"

"Not in the least."

"What do you want me to do, Rodney?"

"Only what you want to do, Julia."

She cried at him, "But Rodney, I don't know what I want to do!"

His voice came back very clear and firm. "Dearest, I shall not tell you what to do. Let's say goodbye until this evening, and you can tell me what you did."

"But Rodney—"

"Just remember—whatever you do, I love you."

She heard the click of the receiver. He had gone. She started to dial impatiently and then she, too, hung up. Very well, she would do what she wanted to do. She would go and have luncheon with Harry.

. . . She went, wearing her violets on the bosom of her gray wool suit. Harry was there waiting for her. He came forward, looking, she saw, very much what he used to be, an impetuous boy. It was only when he was close to her that she saw he had grown older. His blond hair was thinner and there were lines about his blue eyes. He was a good deal heavier, but his suit was cleverly cut to hide it. He put out his hand and she heard the old heartiness of his voice.

"Well, Julia!"

"Hello, Harry!"

They touched hands and she drew hers away quickly.

Yes, it was repulsive to her to touch his hand after all these years. His hand was soft and too smooth. She thought gratefully of Rodney's hand, thin and hard. But how silly of her, as if Harry could help his fair, soft skin! One of Meira's charms was the softness of her skin, inherited from Harry.

"You look wonderful, Julia."

"I'm very happy, Harry. I am going to be married."

She had made up her mind to tell him at once, so that from the knowledge they could speak. He had been married for years. He had children whom she had never seen.

There was the slightest pause before he answered heartily from across the table where they had seated themselves in an alcove. "That's fine. Who is the lucky man?"

"Rodney Meldan," she said.

"Don't know him!" Harry said. "But that doesn't mean anything. I don't know anybody here anymore."

He ordered their luncheon quickly, the same luncheon he used to order. "You see I don't forget," he said smiling.

"How we used to fight about that," she said calmly. They had fought because they were so poor, and steak and mushrooms used up their food allowance for a week.

"Enjoy it, will you?" he retorted. "You have nothing to do with the bill today."

Then he, too, remembered why they had quarreled.

"You used to say you had rather starve all week and have what you wanted once a week, and I said that I had rather have enough of something else all the time than enough only once of this."

"I'm still the same," he said, grinning at her suddenly.

"I believe you are," she said, and laughed. He was

very attractive, this father of her child, if one did not have to be married to him. His blue eyes were as gay as ever, and his mouth as willful. There were signs of his old temper in his ruddy face and hearty voice.

"How's Meira?" he asked.

She felt uncomfortably close to him suddenly at the mention of the child they had had together.

"Oh, Meira," she said lightly, "she's very grown up. She seems to have no more to do with us—eighteen, and in love with a nice young man."

"In love!" he exclaimed, and put down his fork. "Why, she's too young for that."

"So I tell her," she said, toying with a mushroom. "The truth is, Harry, that's the only reason I came today. I wanted to speak about it with you. They told me only last night, and I said immediately what you say—they're too young. I told them a little about us, just to prove it."

He had taken up his fork again. "That's right," he said. "You were just eighteen—I proposed at the birthday party, didn't I? And we were married the next day. I never could wait for what I wanted."

"Meira was born before I was nineteen," she said.

"Gosh, how we used to fight over her," he said half-ruefully.

"Was there anything we didn't fight over?" she said, lifting her eyelashes at him.

"Don't," he said sharply.

"Don't what?"

"Look at me like that!"

"Sorry," she said. "I didn't mean to look at you at all."

They did not speak for a moment. Then he began rather formally, "My own daughter—that is, my daughter Joyce—will be fourteen very soon. I've been thinking too long of her as a baby. But they grow fast."

"You have two children, haven't you?" she asked.

"Three," he said. "My wife and I are very fond of children." He might have been a stranger, but she knew him too well. A small smile pulled at her lips. He was afraid of himself and so he put on formality to protect himself. She resisted the mischievous temptation to laugh aloud. "That's nice," she said politely. "I always thought you'd make a good father—to some other woman's children."

He glanced at her doubtfully, and she gave up her pretense and laughed. "Let's be frank with one another," she said. "We don't care a bit about each other. I'm very much in love with Rodney. You've had years of being married to a nice woman."

"Eve's been wonderful," he said shortly.

"Good!" she said. "I'm glad. Now, let's talk about Meira."

He took a drink of the red wine he had ordered, and wiped his lips. "What sort of a fellow is this—this—what's his name?"

"A good boy," she said, "hardworking, a job in his father's law firm. But he's jealous—I can see that."

She wondered if he would remember how jealous he had been in those old days. They had quarreled about his jealousy of her every look and gesture until sometimes she had thrown herself upon the bed to weep with anger.

"What's he jealous for if she's promised to marry him?" he asked.

"She's very pretty, Harry."

"Is she? You mean so that every other fellow wants to get near her?"

"She can't help that," she said.

"I'm not so sure," he growled. "It's my notion that women can help that sort of thing if they want to."

Ah, she thought, he doesn't remember! She smiled. "What does your wife think about that?" she asked.

"Eve? Oh, Eve's as straight as a string. I never worry about her. She wouldn't look at anybody else."

I never looked at anybody either, her heart protested. But she kept silence. And Eve, was she beautiful? Probably not! But it could not be asked.

Harry said solemnly, "And at our age, Eve's and mine, we don't of course think of that sort of thing."

She did not answer this. Then after a moment she said, "We do agree then that Meira is too young?"

"Meira," he repeated, and suddenly he laughed. "I have to laugh when I hear you say that name. Remember, I wanted to call her Susan, after my mother?"

"I didn't want her called after anybody," she said.

"Will you tell me now where you got that name Meira?" he asked with an echo of his old scorn.

"I told you, I made it up," she said with heat.

"You said that, but I didn't believe you. It's a silly name."

"Curiously, it suits her," she said coldly. "Perhaps I felt that it did even then," she added.

"Still have your old intuitions, eh?" he asked.

She did not answer this. Then she said with impatience, "Shall I tell Meira that you think she is too young?"

"Want me to tell her, Julia?"

"Do you want to see her, Harry?"

She said to herself that now she did not care whether he saw Meira or not. Once it had been fury and pain to her that he did not want to see his own child. He had married so quickly, so shamefully soon, after the divorce.

He looked at her and she saw alarm in his eyes. "What do you want me to do, Julia?"

"I don't care what you do, Harry."

He reflected a moment. "I don't believe Eve would like it. We never talk about you or Meira."

Her voice came very cool and dry. "I certainly couldn't advise you to do something she didn't like."

His ruddy face turned a deeper red. "As a matter of fact—perhaps I ought to—the truth is, she's always been jealous of you."

She laughed at that, a clear, frank laugh, too. "Oh, poor Harry!"

But he did not smile. "Better let things be as they are," he said gravely. "Anyway, it might upset Meira, too—my barging into her life now."

"Perhaps," she agreed.

They waited for their dessert and he lit her cigarette. The flame of his lighter shone on his face. She saw for a moment the passionate boy she had once loved. Did she regret it? She was not sure she did.

"What was the matter with us, Harry?" she asked. Her voice was soft, and she leaned toward him on her elbows.

"You mean—why didn't we make a go of it?"

"Yes."

He drew hard on his own cigarette. "Well," he said, "I've often asked myself that. We had everything, you might say—I had a job and the promise of a raise. That was a cute house, wasn't it? I've often thought of the workshop I had in the basement. I've never had as good a one since."

"You were handsome," she said.

"You were pretty," he retorted.

They both laughed and suddenly all need to fence with each other was gone. They could remember those two they had once been, and whom they were no more.

"I don't know why I used to get so angry with you," she said gaily. "I was terribly in love with you, and then suddenly it seemed to me I hated you just as terribly."

"I was crazy about you, and then suddenly I wanted to hit you all the time," he said. "The trouble was we couldn't agree on anything."

"That was the trouble," she said, remembering. "You never hung up your clothes, and you always waked the baby when you came into the house."

"But gosh, I hadn't seen you all day!" he expostulated.

"You were a Republican and I was a Democrat—still am," she said.

"So am I still a Republican," he said firmly.

"You came home drunk the night Harding was elected."

"I didn't the night Coolidge was elected," he retorted.

"I wouldn't have cared what you did then!"

They laughed again and enjoyed their gaiety.

"You wanted both windows up at night no matter what the weather was," he said.

"I can't bear being stuffy," she said.

"And I wanted you to wear red—"

"I couldn't wear red all the time!" she cried.

She laughed and wiped her eyes with her handkerchief. "Oh, dear," she sighed, "how silly we were—such children, Harry! We hadn't any business being married."

"None in the world," he agreed.

"What we fought about," she said musing, "such small things, so childish. And neither of us would ever give up anything for the other. Yet was there anything about me that you really didn't like, Harry?"

"Nothing," he said. "I always liked you and I like you now."

"So do I like you," she said impulsively, and felt as

safe as though a wall stood between them. She did not love him in the least. They had been too long separated. Love had died in anger, and had not risen again.

"Did we ever love each other, do you think, Harry?"

He considered this. "Yes, we did, Julia, as far as we knew how."

She turned this over in her mind. "That's rather wise of you, Harry. I think you're right. We really did the best we knew. Was there anything else wrong except youth?"

"Honestly, I don't think there was," he said.

"What's the moral of that, Harry?"

"I don't know, Julia—except that maybe, if we hadn't been so young, we'd have stuck it out longer and got to know each other better. When you're so young, I guess you matter more to yourself than anybody else matters, and what you think matters more than what anybody else thinks."

She saw his mind beginning to turn from their past. It was dead, and their brief meeting had not revived it except for a moment. He was motioning for the waiter and she began to put on her gloves.

"Then, Harry, shall I tell Meira to go ahead?"

He counted his change and left an extravagant tip. That, she thought, was always what he used to do. "I don't want to advise you, Julia," he said. "I have been out of touch so long. Whatever you do I shall approve. I've always approved your good sense."

He was suddenly so changed, so middle-aged, that she wondered how she had ever thought him like the young Harry she had once married. He was looking at his watch. "I must hurry, I'm afraid. I have to catch a train. They're expecting me at home tonight. One of the boys is graduating from grammar school."

He smiled, appealing for her understanding, and she gave it quickly. "Of course," she said, "you mustn't disappoint them."

She rose, put out her hand, and he took it warmly. She did not mind at all the touch of it now. It was a stranger's hand, after all, someone whom she had known, briefly, when they were young.

"Goodbye, Harry."

"Goodbye, Julia. Let me know what Meira decides. I'd like to send her a present if she gets married."

She did not wait while he found his hat. She went quickly into the street and took a cab home. The house was very quiet when she entered it and she was glad. She wanted to be quite alone for a while until she knew what the meeting meant for her—for Meira. It had been so like Harry to throw back the responsibility upon her. That was what he used to do about everything.

She went up to her own room and lay upon the long chair up near the window. From here she could see the garden all clear color in the afternoon sunlight. It was as she loved it best, shadow and sunlight distinct, and each hue itself. Then in the painstaking deliberation which was her way of thought she went over the hour she had spent with Harry. She might so easily have been married to him now, had they both been more patient. But they had been impatient, and so they had parted, and their lives had gone on until now they were separate, so separate indeed that she could feel nothing, neither pain nor regret. It was like a dream, those two years they had once lived together. By so small a chance as their young impatience had the world changed for them. And she did not care anymore. The bright afternoon sun made her drowsy and her lids drooped and she was asleep.

When she woke the sun was low and she sat up quickly. What time was it? Why, she had been asleep for hours! It was ten minutes to five and in less than an hour Rodney would be here. She leaped from her chair and hurried to bathe and to dress. She was suddenly hungry for Rodney, she wanted to see him, to touch him, to make sure that he was all that he had been yesterday. She felt rested and happy and she sang softly under her breath as she put on a violet chiffon that was Rodney's favorite. She was beautiful—she saw that without vanity as she brushed her hair, more beautiful perhaps than she had ever been in her life. She was glad of it for Rodney's sake—yes, and for her own. It was joyful to be married when one was at one's most beautiful.

She went downstairs a little early and as she was coming down the steps she heard Meira's voice from the library. She went in and found the two of them, Robert and Meira, sitting solemnly side by side on the couch. They rose when she came in.

"We've been waiting ages for you," Meira said tensely. "I looked in your room and saw you asleep, so we waited. We wanted you to know first of all—"

Rob leaned toward her and pulled her arms and then for the first time Julia saw that Meira's left hand was behind her back. "Let her see it," Rob said.

Meira held out her hand. There upon her finger was the ring, a thin platinum band. "We decided to be married right off," she said.

"Oh, Meira!" Julia gasped. She sank down upon a chair.

"We were afraid we'd get to quarreling about whether we ought to or not," Meira said, "and the best way to agree on it was simply to do it—"

"Oh," Julia whispered, "oh, but—" It was on her tongue to cry out, "But, Meira, that's so exactly what Harry and I did!"

Yes, that was how it had happened the day after the party. They had argued, she against and he for, and suddenly he had closed her mouth with kisses. "If you start quarreling with me about this," he had said, "we'll never get married at all. So we're going to get married now."

And she had gone home to her parents and told them that night and her mother had cried.

"But, Mother, I have the right," she had said to her mother over and over.

"After all, Mother, I have the right to marry Rob if I want to," Meira was saying.

She rose swiftly and went over to kiss her daughter. "Of course you have," she said. Then she kissed Rob's cheek. "You have the right to everything," she said. "At your age," she added.

"Oh, Mother," Meira cried, "I knew you'd see it!"

They were gone in a moment, clasping each other's waists—children, children, she thought, as she and Harry had once been. But suddenly she knew she was not sorry for that marriage of hers with Harry. They had been too young, that was all. But there was nothing to be sorry about.

She sat down at the piano and began to play softly, and then stopped because she heard Rodney's footsteps. She turned and saw him, very tall, and coming toward her. She could not tell from his face what he was thinking. He looked as he always did, faithful and steadfast and good, his eyes dark under the graying hair. He bent and kissed her. Had she met him when she was eighteen would she have loved him instead of Harry? It was an idle question—they had not met until a year ago and she was only glad that she was free. Life went on and one accepted what it brought.

"Are you all right?" he asked, looking down into her face.

"Perfectly," she said, looking up into his. "Harry's so much what he always was, Rodney. I'm glad I saw him. It makes me love you more."

"Good," he said. He put his hands upon her cheeks and she felt them strong and steady.

"Meira's married," she said suddenly. "To Rob—today, without telling anyone."

He continued to search her soul with his dark eyes. "You approve?" he asked.

"They have to live where they are," she said. "Doesn't everybody?"

"Yes," he said, slowly, "here and now." He drew her to her feet and held her close for a long moment.

"You weren't angry with me today?" she asked at last.

"Angry?" he repeated. "How could I be angry with you? I love you."

She gazed at him. Yes, he was speaking the truth. He loved her better than he loved himself and that was why he would never be angry with her. "I only want you to have what you want," he said with a sort of gentle diffidence. "That is what I think love means."

At our age, she thought, and did not speak the words.

Instead, other words came tumbling to her lips. She had not planned them but there they were in her mind—they must have been, for the sight of his face at this moment drew them out of her.

"Rodney, I've changed my mind. Please, I do want to be married—not Thursday, but tomorrow!"

He looked startled. "But darling—darling!" She saw he was perplexed with her change.

"But, please, Rodney, will you marry me tomorrow!"

He seized her in his arms again and buried his face in her neck. "Oh, Julia—but are you sure?"

"Do you want to marry me, Rodney?"

"Do I want to marry you! I've been scared to death all day."

"Oh, Rodney, have you? But you didn't tell me—"

"I'm telling you now—scared to death—trying to make up my mind to be ready for anything." He lifted his head. "Though I was going to put up a fight for myself, Julia!"

"There never was any need for that fight, Rodney."

"Tomorrow, in the morning, Julia—let's be married in the morning!"

"In the morning," she promised him.

She drew away from him at last and began to laugh silently, her head against his shoulder. He lifted her head with his hand under her chin, inquiring with his eyes of that laughter.

"What will Meira say?" she asked. "What will she and Rob say to us?"

"Do we need to ask them?"

"No," she said, "nobody needs to ask anybody anything, so far as I can see," and she put her head again upon his shoulder.

Morning in the Park

IT HAD BEEN SO LONG since Margaret Lambert had been in New York that now, on one of the first days of an early spring, she felt faintly stifled. It might be perhaps the tall buildings, which showed so narrow a sky; it might be only her own garments, which sat stiffly on her slender body, used to the ease of country clothes. She felt her breath come short, whatever the reason, and with the necessity to stay overnight, because she could not get the appointment she needed with her oculist until the next day, she abandoned her thought of a matinee. Stopping a cab, she directed the driver to Central Park. There at least she would find space about her, and she would sit for a little while in quiet.

In this fashion she happened to be in the park at the time of late morning when the nurses and nannies of New York's best families sun and air their charges. She took her seat beyond the small important circle, partly because it was in the most pleasant part of the park and partly because she loved little children, and with no prospect of having any of her own, she allowed herself to enjoy the children of others when she had opportunity. There had been times, since she and Bertram had parted, now nearly six years ago, when it had been a true temptation to marry one of the two men who wanted to marry her, in order that she might have children of her own. She had dallied with this temptation, but had never quite yielded to it, on the pretended ground that she could not make up her mind which man to marry. She might close her eyes and put out her hand and let chance decide. Actually she was too just a woman to marry a man merely for a home and children. Plenty of women did, but she could not.

So she had continued to live in the small farmhouse where she and Bertram had chosen to live because it was so far away from anyone they knew. They had made no friends and after Bertram went away she had continued to live without friends, and quite alone. There was no reason to cultivate the farm families who were her neighbors beyond the pleasant small talk over the purchase of eggs and milk and an occasional chicken. She had her painting and once a year, as now, she brought her pictures to New York and held a modest exhibition at one of the smaller galleries. Slowly she had made a slight fame for herself as a painter of country landscapes, and she needed very little to live upon. Bertram had been generous in saying that his share in what they had paid together for the house was to be hers. Neither of them had spoken what each had thought, that since he was marrying a rich woman, he need not think of money anymore.

Margaret breathed deeply. Here in the park the air was quite good—a sea breeze perhaps? She had forgotten how to catch directions in the city. Her little house faced east and in the country by turning her face in imagination toward her front door she could always know where she was. But there was a goodish patch of sky over the park, and most of it was blue. The sun came brilliantly from behind a cloud at this moment. The children, during the space of the last quarter of an hour when the sun had been behind a cloud, had seemed listless and silent. Now when the sun fell on them they sprang into life, and Margaret, smiling, put aside all other thoughts to watch them.

One little girl out of the dozen or so children was easily spectacular. She was not more than three, or three and a half, but she was already an accomplished individual. Her rose-pink coat and bonnet were trimmed with narrow bands of white fur and she swung a tiny white fur muff. Her hair and eyes were dark and her skin was warm and brown. Sunlamps, Margaret supposed, took the place of summer sun, or it might be that she had been in Florida. People came back about now for the spring. She was an amusingly naughty little girl, and her nanny reproved her often.

"Now, Miss Beatrice, have done, do!" The middle-aged Englishwoman spoke these words every few minutes.

Miss Beatrice pouted and dropped her long eyelashes and began to suck her thumb, which Nanny plucked out of her mouth.

"Whatever would your mummy say, if she should come now, which I am expecting her every minute, you naughty girl?"

Miss Beatrice threw her white muff on the walk and pushed the baby carriage which Nanny had been guarding. This resulted in Nanny's firmly setting her on the seat beside her and remarking that of all the little gals she had ever taken care of in London, including Lady Marcia Stanley's little ones, she had never seen so difficult a child as Miss Beatrice.

"It's the American atmosphere," she told the other nurses, who were watching coldly. "Children aren't allowed—not in England—but whatever can one do if the parents encourage the children?" Parents, the nurses agreed, were the bane of their lives and the ruination of children.

While this conversation was going on Margaret caught Miss Beatrice's eyes, and they indulged in a long mutual stare. Margaret smiled, but Miss Beatrice was grave. Suddenly she slipped off the seat, for the push had waked the baby in the perambulator, and ran to Margaret without being noticed.

"Who's you?" Miss Beatrice inquired.

The nurses combined in informing Miss Beatrice's nanny what had happened. The Englishwoman looked hastily around.

"It's quite all right," Margaret said in her quiet voice. "Do let her stay for a bit. I'm fond of children."

Her accents were those of a lady, and Nanny hesitated. "We should be going along," she murmured.

At this Miss Beatrice screamed, "I won't!" The white muff came into play again. Miss Beatrice flung it far away straight in the path of a small boy who was riding a tricycle. Nanny rushed for it.

"You don't like the muff, I see," Margaret observed.

"I do like my muff," Miss Beatrice said willfully.

"Yet you throw it about," Margaret hinted.

" 'Cause I like to make Nanny run fas'," Miss Beatrice confided with a lovely smile.

They interchanged a delicious secret look and then Miss Beatrice dug her round elbows into Margaret's knee. "Wha's you name?" she inquired with much charm.

"Meg," Margaret replied.

Now how could that name rise to her lips so simply? No one had spoken it since Bertram went away.

"Meg—Meg—Meggie—" Miss Beatrice chanted.

"Do you come here every morning?" Margaret inquired hastily.

"I come ever mawnin' unless I goes to beaches," Miss Beatrice replied, "Or ceptin' rain."

Nanny had now fetched back the muff. The little boy had rolled it some distance and she returned red and displeased. "Miss Beatrice, come along, now, do," she said in a firm voice which ignored Margaret. "Your mummy will be here—"

"The's Mummy," Miss Beatrice remarked. She pointed a forefinger at an extremely pretty young woman who was walking rapidly toward them. Nanny pulled Miss Beatrice sharply away toward the perambulator and put her little hands into the muff.

"Are you ready, Nanny?" the pretty woman cried in a brisk, somewhat imperious voice. "I'm sorry I'm late. My fitting took longer than I thought."

"Quite ready, madame," Nanny said.

Miss Beatrice took the opportunity to throw down her muff yet again.

"Beatrice!" her mother said sharply. "Pick up your muff!"

Miss Beatrice did not move and Nanny picked it up. "She's has been adoin' of that this whole blessed mornin', madame."

"But why?" the pretty woman asked.

Miss Beatrice did not reply. She looked quite impassive and then discovered another subject. "Look at wee tiny bu'd," she suggested. A robin sat upon a shrub nearby.

"Come along—come along," her mother cried in her high, clear voice, "We can't keep the car waiting or the policeman will get us." She took the little girl's hand and

Nanny in haste pushed the perambulator. Some clock nearby tolled the hour of noon and one by one the nurses went away. The little group of rich children were gone.

Margaret continued to sit immobile upon the bench. She was aware of sunlight and silence. The roar of the city was subdued but near. Her senses of sound and sight were quickened by country living, and yet she felt unable to move or to respond. For she had recognized the pretty woman. She was Bertram's wife.

"Of course she is pretty?" she had said to Bertram. It was her first answer to what she had divined he was trying to tell her. She had long known herself not beautiful. Her artist's eye had been quietly content with her few good points, a good figure proudly carried, a well-shaped head and mouth. But the combination did not make beauty. Her hair was abundant but colorless and her eyes were gray and her features were heavy. There was no use pretending and neither of them ever did. She had been large-minded enough to take pleasure in the beauty of other women, when Bertram admired one or another in passing, and she had been surprised at her own quick question.

"Sandra's considered beautiful," he had said briefly.

It had happened on a late evening in October. Could she not remember? He had come home rather late, but she had made him walk with her along the edge of the small brook in the woods behind the house. The leaves were dropping, still gold and red, and the brown woods water carried them away. She was always exalted by the sense of change in the year. Spring and autumn, when the earth turned, were times of renewal for her spirit. But Bertram that day had seemed melancholy and restless. He had scarcely answered her, and when they reached the fallen oak she had sat down.

"Come, Bertram," she had said. "Out with it. What's on your mind?"

"Something I hate to tell you and yet I must," he had replied.

She had always supposed that she would know when the moment of parting came but stupidly she had not recognized it. It was her own fault. He had never proposed marriage to her and she had not insisted upon it—perhaps had not wanted it, feeling his hidden instability and wanting to keep her proud independence. Now he did not sit down beside her and she sat looking up at him. He was neither tall nor short, and dark rather than fair. But there was something charming about his changeful, irregular looks. Sometimes he was strikingly handsome, and sometimes he was plain. What he was depended upon his mood, and his mood, as she had learned, depended upon external circumstances. A pleasant review of one of his books could make him brilliant and charming for an evening. A little money that he had not expected from some sale abroad made him gay and generous for a few days. But to borrow money of her, as he sometimes was compelled to do, made him almost hate her.

She had pondered often on how she could supply his bank account without his knowing it. For though she never had spectacular success and neither he nor she was under any delusion about her moderate talent, yet her small sales were steady. Tourists passing by quite often bought one of her little canvases, and she kept her prices within their reach. She had no ambitions except to live in happiness. So it was she who always had money, though never more than a little, and he who had stretches of nothing at all. These were the arid times, the times when some small meanness in him could astonish her, and this she could bear less easily than his monstrous, unreasonable irritations. At first she had been bewildered by his unjust furies with her, as for example when he did not like the way she prepared eggs for their supper. She was not too good a cook and he was a better one, but whether he would help her depended also upon his mood. On that day he had jumped up from his chair, and taking the dish of eggs, he had emptied them into the fire. She had sat quite still while he snarled at her, "Dried leather—"

He was abjectly sorrowful after these irritations were gone. At first she had tenderly received his sorrow and had forgotten the anger. But as time went on she felt a slight thickening about her heart. At last she felt neither his anger nor his repentance, and learned to accept him whole and as he was, a creature of volatile good and evil.

And why had she not known that the moment had come that October evening? She was, she supposed, a simple creature, taking it for granted that he felt the same loyalty to her that she did to him, taking it for granted that he loved her as she loved him. Had they not been together for eleven years? She was thirty-five and he thirty-seven—certainly not young anymore. She had taken it for granted that their relationship was settled, even in its independence. So she was not in the least prepared.

She had said with the instinctive patience which she had learned, "How can there be anything which you can't tell me?"

He had darted at her one of his strange, strong looks, and as though he took courage from the calm in her eyes, he had said abruptly, "Well, then—I want to get married!"

Even then she had not seen what he meant. By some stupidity she thought that he wanted now to make their union permanent in marriage. A deep flush rose from her breast to her neck and her cheeks.

"Do you think we'd be happier?" she had said half-timidly. She felt almost shy at this mention of marriage after so many years.

Then instantly she saw her mistake. He had turned quite pale.

"Do forgive me," he had said almost formally. "I didn't mean—us."

She had collected herself. "Stupid of me," she said quickly. "I didn't think—"

"Not at all," he had urged.

"But of course," she had said, strangling, "we're both free—"

He had broken through this defense which each had put up. He sat down beside her and he spoke gently and reasonably. "It's not 'of course,' at all, Meg," he had said. "It's perfect agony for me. You and I, after all these years—"

He reached for her hand and she did not refuse it. But she could not speak. So he went on.

"I can't see the end of—of living like this."

"Must there be an end?" she had whispered. Try as she could, her voice would not come from her throat with any strength.

"Well, I do want more out of life somehow," he had said. "I don't want more from any woman, Meg. I know that there can't be more than you've given me."

"Not enough—" She had managed these two words.

"Everything," he had said generously and swiftly, "but it just isn't in your power—or mine, it seems—to go beyond—this—"

This, his dark eyes implied, sweeping the few acres, meant the little brook, the small house on the low hillside. She knew what he felt. He longed for life. He wanted travel and experience. He had said sometimes with frequent wistfulness that he would like to know this one and that one among the famous and the great.

"I need to enlarge my world," he said. "I feel restless and stifled here and it makes me bad—Meg, you know it does!"

"I don't think you're bad." She got this out more easily.

"Well, I'm not the man I want to be," he said with the occasional honesty which could charm her so wholly. "If I hadn't to worry about money and sales I could write better books, and then I'd be a much better man."

"I think that's true," she said with some surprise. "It's clever of you to see yourself so clearly, Bertram."

"Oh, I don't know myself," he had said, half laughing. Their hands had fallen apart, and he did not notice it.

"I suppose—it hasn't worked—our love, I mean."

"It has worked," he said warmly. "It's been wonderful—I couldn't have lived without you. I'll never forget you—how could I?"

She had scarcely heard this. Within her mind she was busy with herself. Of course she could get along. Of course she would. She might have made some struggle, have cried some protest, if he had not so cleverly said exactly the right words that, given a different place in the world, he could be a good man. To this her own heart added, possibly even a great one.

She had risen from the log. Twilight had fallen and she could no longer see the color of the leaves on the water. But she could hear the rushing of the brook away from where they stood. "Do you mind going back to town tonight, Bertram?" she had asked quietly.

"And leave you alone?" he had cried, looking up at her.

Then she had said straight out of her instincts. "It wouldn't be quite decent for you to stay here anymore, now."

In the park she looked at her watch. It was nearly two o'clock and the park was almost empty. The sun was strong and pigeons were toddling about searching for food. Across the sidewalk from her an old man sat with a bag of crumbs in his hand making a game with the birds. When they gathered about him he pretended to be asleep. But the birds waited, their eyes fixed on the bag, and he opened one eye and winked at Margaret.

"Can't fool them," he said in glee.

He opened the bag and scattered a handful of crumbs and then screwed the bag up again. The pigeons pushed and pecked at each other and in a few seconds the crumbs were gone.

"But they know when the bag is empty," the old man cried happily. "Damn their little hides, lady, as soon as the bag's empty they go away and don't bother with me. And just let me come without a bag and they don't bother with me, neither. Oh, they know their oats, pigeons does!"

Margaret smiled and rose. "They're pretty, even though they're so greedy."

"They are," the old man said fondly. "That plum-colored fellow now, with the silver wash on his back— handsome, ain't he? He's the greediest one, bless him!"

She smiled again and walked slowly away. Since she had decided to stay in town she might perhaps come back to the park. If it were a clear day the children would be there again.

The next day dawned clear. Though it was only early April the air was warm and a pencil of sunshine reached even into the hotel room. Margaret woke late, for she had not slept well. She had gone to the theater in the evening but the play had not absorbed her. Underneath the rootless stage situation her mind kept delving deep into memory. After she had gone to bed the play was almost dim. But she saw herself and Bertram with dreadful clarity.

He had gone away that night and had left her, as she had asked him to do, and in the empty house she had set things right for the night, had wound the clock and taken the dog out and then had lain in her bed, hour after hour, the light blazing, a book upright in her hands unread. So must all the nights of her life now pass.

She knew Bertram so well. He had risen from a murky childhood in a New York slum, and he had hated his childhood so much that he had never been willing to go back even to show her the tenement house which had been his home. He had left his family altogether, or perhaps it had simply scattered after his mother had died. His father had been a miner for years before he, the youngest child, was born, and had at last been obliged to leave the mines because of silicosis. The only bit that Bertram had told her was about his father, fighting for breath in his hardened lungs, his eyes bulging and full of tears. After he was dead the mother had been a scrubwoman, and the children had run the streets.

Something in the little boy which Bertram had been had kept him alive to hatred of the two dingy rooms, the crowded streets, the wild, neglected street children. He had struggled on, getting out of it when his mother died, getting work for himself in a newspaper office, getting to night school, getting a better job on the paper, trying to write. But he had struggled without confidence in himself. He still had no confidence. All Margaret's love for him, her steady small income, ready if he needed it, had not been enough to give him confidence. Toward dawn after that October night, she had perceived with tragic clarity that only money could give him confidence— plenty of money.

On this April morning in New York she sighed, got out of bed, and since it was warm she decided to wear her new heather-blue spring suit. She had bought it only a few days ago, had worn it to her modest opening, and had enjoyed thinking that it became her. "Oh, Miss Lambert," some woman had cried, "you have put your own calm into your pictures, and that's why I love them."

She had smiled, knowing that no answer was needed. Now, she bathed and brushed out her long straight hair and wound it around her head. She always dressed carefully. In the old days when she and Bertram had made a home together she had often been careless. Now she could not be. There was no one to keep herself up for— except herself. She was her own guest, her own critic. So when she had put on her blue suit and the rather large hat which softened her firm features she looked at herself in the mirror and was pleased, quite without vanity, that she had made the best of herself. Then she went in search for breakfast. Country bred as she was, she liked breakfast, and she ate a substantial one in the hotel dining room, which was nearly empty. Lingering over coffee and cigarette she let an hour pass, so that when she rose to go to the park it was almost ten o'clock.

The children were all there when she reached the bench upon which she had sat yesterday. Fortunately no one else was there, perhaps because the children were lively this morning and a good deal of shrill chatter was going on, against which the nurses raised their own voices in order to transmit absorbing details of gossip.

Miss Beatrice was playing with a new doll and for a moment she did not look up. When she did, she gave a dazzling smile, which Margaret recognized as Bertram's own.

"I don't have any muff," Miss Beatrice called. "Too hot, my mummy says. I has to wait until some snow comes nex' Chris'mus."

Miss Beatrice wore a cream-colored silk coat and a smart little turned-up hat of the same material, her socks were white, and her shoes black patent leather.

"You look beautiful this morning," Margaret said.

"Yes!" Miss Beatrice agreed, "and so is my dolly." She held up her elaborate doll. It was a baby, complete with a nursing bottle full of water at its mouth. "Look," Miss Beatrice confided. "It's just like Bertie—he drinks down some watah and nen—" She lifted the doll's skirts triumphantly.

"Wonderful," Margaret agreed gravely.

Nanny turned hastily. "Miss Beatrice, you stay here," she said with some violence.

Miss Beatrice gave her fascinating smile, "Meggie—Meggie," she said caressingly and, putting down her doll, she moved toward Margaret.

"I hope you won't mind her making friends with me," Margaret said quietly.

Nanny wavered. "She mustn't bother."

"Oh no," Margaret agreed.

So Miss Beatrice crossed the three or four feet to Margaret's side and stood with her elbows digging comfortably again into Margaret's knees. "Know who I am?" she inquired.

"Who are you?" Margaret asked.

"Beatrice Louise Marie Westcott!"

"Nice names," Margaret murmured.

"Mummy gived me her name—is Beatrice, and Grandme're Louise and Grandme're Marie gived me their names, too."

"And Bertie?" Margaret asked. Marie had been Bertram's mother's name.

"He's a boy," Miss Beatrice said with reserve.

"And he has just one name?" Margaret asked.

"Daddy gived him two names, is Bert'am Roger, and he has Westcott, too, like me."

"Nice," Margaret murmured.

There was a strong shout from the perambulator and Nanny hastily shifted the hood and propped up a fat baby. Miss Beatrice put her finger in her mouth and sucked it for a moment while she watched him. "There's Bertie," she said somewhat coldly.

Bertie sat upright with effort and stared around him. He had been sleeping on his right cheek and it was crimson. His eyes were bright blue and staring and he held his mouth slightly open. Obviously he had not yet adjusted himself to a waking world.

"Bertie don't know nuffin," Miss Beatrice said disparagingly. "He just can eat and sleep and gets mad."

"Really?" Margaret exclaimed.

"An' I can say A B C halfway and I can count my fingers and toeses—not together but first fingers and then toeses."

"Of course Bertie is younger," Margaret offered.

"When I was little I could do it, too," Miss Beatrice assured her. "My daddy said so."

"Your daddy?" Margaret asked. Oh, wicked woman, and foolish!

"My daddy likes me best and I like him best," Miss

Beatrice said fondly. "He even likes me best of my mummy, cause he says so. He says he likes me best of any ladies in the world."

Miss Beatrice waved both arms vigorously in circles. "The world is like this," she explained, "round and round. My daddy says so."

"Do you believe everything he tells you?" Margaret inquired.

Miss Beatrice opened large dark eyes. "'Cause he don't tell me lies," she affirmed.

She leaned on Margaret's knees again. "And you know what? Eve'y day he plays house with me. I cook his supper on my stove. And he says is the best supper he has."

"What does your daddy do?" Margaret asked. How hateful was she, prying open a child!

"He writes big books, and Mummy buys 'em and she puts on some pwetty pwetty red covahs, some gold on, and when I am big I s'all read my daddy's books—"

"Miss Beatrice!" Nanny called. "Come and get your sandwich!"

Miss Beatrice broke off. "So long," she said pleasantly.

Nanny cried out in horror. "Miss Beatrice, don't you dare say that to the lady!" She turned severe eyes to Margaret. "You wouldn't think, now, how she picks up the talk from the elevator man. Madame does get that upset, and her father too—a real gentleman, though he's American."

Margaret smiled coolly. "The child seems fond of him." Meanwhile Miss Beatrice munched a bread-and-butter sandwich, interlaid with thin slices of apple.

"So she should be," Nanny said stoutly. "A good father and a wonderful man. He devotes himself to those two. In the morning, of course, he writes—a great writer he is, whose name you'd doubtless know—but then with all Madame's money—" Nanny pursed her lips and lifted her eyebrows.

Margaret smiled again, pretending no interest.

"Miss Beatrice, wipe your hands on the napkin—do!" Nanny cried with passion.

Miss Beatrice touched her hands to a small linen napkin and Nanny poured a cup of milk from a thermos. "Now I shall hold it," she said, but Miss Beatrice held it also, drinking the milk slowly and gazing at Margaret over the rim of the silver cup.

"It's so nice to see a happy family these days," Margaret said.

"It is that," Nanny said heartily. With Miss Beatrice fed she turned her attention to Bertie, who guzzled his milk bottle greedily, his eyes slightly out of focus as he stared concentratedly at nothing.

Miss Beatrice, sated, now sat down on a small folding stool and undressed her doll. And Margaret sat quietly in the sunshine. The children were beautifully dressed, perfectly tended. Bertram would enjoy that. He had a feeling for perfection in details. The perambulator was massively English, the robes were of satin, silk-lined, and heavily monogrammed. Even Miss Beatrice's little bag was handmade and monogrammed in graceful, feathery letters. Well, Bertram might go to excess in perfection. He did not like homespun, she remembered. There was a trace of something in him—a tinge of the exotic.

He had of course come back the next day after the night when she had sent him away. He had not gone back to town—only to the nearest village hotel, where it seemed the proprietor had stared at him but had asked no questions.

Bertram had tried to laugh when he told her of it. "I

felt a good deal of a fool," he had said over the breakfast table.

She had not thought of breakfast. She had waked in a daze and had got up without hunger. But when he came in she set about the meal in almost total silence.

"Now look here, Meg," he had said when she had poured his coffee. "You can spoil this for me or you can make it wonderful."

"I don't want to spoil anything for anybody," she had said with stiff lips that she could not control.

"I know you don't," he had said with resolute cheerfulness. "I know how wonderful you are, thank God. What I mean is that I have to feel you approve of what I am doing. After all, we've always agreed that it is right to move toward the place of greatest growth and that is what I am doing. I shall be able perhaps to—to influence her whole family for better things. God knows the world is a mess! And they haven't spent their money too wisely. You know I don't care for money for its own sake."

It was true. He cared for money because having it could set him free. Free from what? From his own evil! Good and evil this man was and she knew it. Had he been born a rich man's son he could have put aside all need for small deceits and vanities and angers. He was capable of living up to an environment. He could be a good rich man even as being a poor man he could stoop amazingly low to make some small gain. She could never forget one dreadful night when they had been together for less than a year. Bertram had won a short story prize. He had come home high with joy, and she had seen for the first time a glimpse of what he could be. Then somehow he had let slip the fact that he had been attacked by another writer, younger than himself, for having stolen the plot of the story.

She had been getting ready for bed when he said this, and she let the hairbrush drop from her hand. "But, Bertram—did you?" She swept back her long hair to see him clearly.

He was sitting on a straight chair, leaning with his arms on the back, watching her and telling her how he had gone up before a great audience to receive the prize.

"Of course I didn't," he exclaimed.

"Then why—"

"Look here, Meg," he had burst forth. "You know that a writer picks up his ideas where he can get them. How did I know the young fool was planning to write the story himself? I thought he was merely telling an incident."

"Who is he?" she had interrupted.

"Kenneth MacLean," he had said sullenly. "And he hasn't a ghost of proof. There was no one there except the two of us."

"Oh, Bertram!" she had groaned.

Later, when she had failed after hours of argument to make him see what he had done, she had given up. She had thought of searching out the young man herself and then she had decided against it. She could not do it. But she could refuse the gold chain and locket that Bertram had wanted to buy for her next day. It was an old-fashioned trinket in the village store. Someone had put it there, wanting cash. When Bertram took it up she shook her head. "Oh, no," she had said for Mr. Fenny's benefit. "We need the money for bread and milk and meat." Bertram had been cross with her when they reached home, but it was for something else. Then at the breakfast table she had remembered it, and she remembered, too, that he had wanted the prize money for her sake. So she said, "Bertram, get this clear in your mind. I think it's the most sensible thing in the world for you to marry Sandra Westcott."

"But—what will you do?" he had muttered belatedly.

"I shall be content," she had replied. Then she had made her supreme effort. "I shall watch you rise from one high place to another, and then I'll know that it was right—"

"If you think I ought to go, I'll do my best. I shan't disappoint you," he had said simply.

"I do," she insisted.

It was incredible that he should have said these words, that he should have taken her hand and kissed it.

But so he had said and done.

"Come, Miss Beatrice," Nanny said imperatively. "We have to go home early today. I have packin' to do. We're goin' on the big ship come Saturday."

"Goin' onna big ship," Miss Beatrice echoed. She threw her smile toward Margaret. "You know we goin' onna big ship?"

"Where will the big ship take you?" Margaret asked playfully.

"Madame has a place in England," Nanny said. She put Bertie down, adjusted the hood, and then noticed that the big doll was nude.

"Oh, for shame, Miss Beatrice!" she cried. "Naughty—naughty! Not a stitch on and so lifelike it's not decent!" She seized the doll and dressed it rapidly. "I can't think why the child always wants to take off and never to put on," she said somewhat peevishly. "Well, now, come along, do, Miss Beatrice!"

"Shall I say goodbye?" Margaret asked.

"Oh, I daresay we'll be here tomorrow, if it's fair," Nanny said carelessly.

"Bye, bye," Miss Beatrice said sweetly. "Meggie, Meggie," she added roguishly. "Meggie—Meggie— Meggie—Meggie—"

Nanny led her away, and Margaret sat watching them. She half hoped that the little girl would turn and wave but she did not. She had both arms about the doll.

THERE WAS REALLY NO REASON why she should return to the little lonely house. She had sold enough pictures to feed her for the next six or seven months and in that time there would be more pictures. Winter was always fertile for her. There was nothing to do but paint all day and at night sit before the fire and listen to music floating in from the air. While she and Bertram had been together she had allowed her old friendships to die, and the friends he had brought her were his, not hers, and he had taken them with him. And the city was behaving well this April day. The afternoon was clear and she spent it on a little steamboat that went around the island. She had never seen the city whole before. It lay like an encrusted jewel in the sea. When she got back she was pleasantly tired and after she had eaten she went to bed with a book and fell asleep soon.

She slept well that night and did not wake early. In the country the birds always woke her early, twittering in the ivy outside her window. She rose feeling unusually content, and at midmorning she sauntered toward the park again. She was disappointed to see someone sitting on her bench—a woman. But she continued her walk toward the children. The big English perambulator was not there nor could she see Miss Beatrice. A foolish depression fell upon her. Was she not to see that adorable child of Bertram's again? Then she saw a tiny female figure, this time in a blue woolen frock and small blue hat, come from behind the bench where the lady sat. It was Miss Beatrice and in a moment Margaret saw that the lady was her mother, Bertram's wife. She could not turn back without being conspicuous. Besides, it was too late. Miss Beatrice had seen her.

"Meggie—Meggie!" she cried in a high, fluty voice.

Mrs. Westcott looked up from a book she was reading. "Hush, Beatrice," she said mildly.

"It's Meggie," Miss Beatrice insisted. She ran and seized Margaret's hand and dragged her to the bench.

Margaret smiled, half yielding. "We've made friends these last few days—"

"It's Mummy," Miss Beatrice said.

"I think you must be Mrs. Westcott," Margaret said. "I'm afraid your little girl has told me about her family."

Mrs. Westcott looked reserved but courteous. "I'm afraid Beatrice is a talkative child. Do come and sit down if I've taken your place."

"It's not my place," Margaret said, still smiling. "I just happened to be about. I'm spending a few days in the city, and not liking the city, the park seemed the nearest thing to the country."

She sat down, however. There was not the slightest sign of recognition in Mrs. Westcott's blue eyes. Was it possible that Bertram had told her nothing whatever of all those years?

Miss Beatrice leaned on Margaret's knees in her accustomed posture. "Bertie got sick," she announced. "He fowed up too much."

Margaret lifted her quiet eyes. "I hope the little boy is not ill?"

"No—only greedy," Mrs. Westcott said with slight impatience. "But really, Beatrice, it was your fault. You shouldn't have given him your biscuit. He eats anything—"

Miss Beatrice looked somewhat wicked. "He tooked it out of my own hand," she explained.

"Nonsense," Mrs. Westcott declared, "as if a baby could take something out of your hand!" She turned to Margaret. "Her father spoils her inexcusably. He will not have her blamed for anything. Consequently she will never say that she is at fault. I don't know what will happen as she grows older."

"She will probably have everything she wants," Margaret said. She smiled down at Miss Beatrice, who responded with warmth by crying out, "I just eat you up!"

Margaret's heart stopped. These were the foolish, playful words which Bertram had used so often.

"Beatrice!" her mother cried. "Don't be silly! That's her father again—he often says he will eat her up."

"It must be wonderful to have such a father," Margaret murmured.

"Oh well," Mrs. Westcott said, "he's a writer and so he says anything—"

"I am sure he means it with this child—" Margaret took the little hand which Miss Beatrice extended.

"I only hope she doesn't expect it from everybody else," Mrs. Westcott said.

She was evidently not going to say any more about Bertram, and Margaret, longing to hear, dared to announce herself. "Since your daughter and I are such friends, I ought to introduce myself. I'm Margaret Lambeth, a painter of mild sorts, and I am having an exhibition—that's why I am here."

"Really?" The pretty woman hesitated a moment. "I'm Mrs. Bertram Westcott—"

"Oh," Margaret exclaimed, "then I know your husband's books. The last one, *King's Men*, I thought was his very best."

Bertram's wife looked complacent. "Yes, he is working very well now, isn't he? He says it's because he's so absolutely happy. He longed for a home of his own always, but—well, he just didn't settle down. So many men are like that, I think. And then it came over him one day what was the matter. He had no roots of his own in life. I'm happy that he didn't know that until he saw me." She paused to laugh rather sweetly. "But it was quite quick with both of us. He's older than I am— ten years! And he wanted children at once. He adores them. He can't bear being away from them and I have a suite of rooms fitted especially for him to work in so that he needn't be interrupted, even though he's at home."

"It's very important to be happy," Margaret said.

"For him it is," Bertram's wife said warmly.

"It must be wonderful for you—to think you make him so happy," Margaret said.

Bertram's wife looked at her from under shy eyelashes. "He's quite wonderful," she acknowledged.

"I'm sure he is," Margaret said in the same quiet voice. "What is he writing now?"

"Oh, he's halfway through his next book—a lovely, sad sort of thing, like music—about a man who loved two women and had to choose between them."

"Why did he have to choose?" How difficult to make the voice casual as though she did not care!

"Well, you see," the sweetly cultivated voice grew earnest. "With one of them he simply couldn't be his best self. And he was unhappy unless he knew he was all that he could be."

Miss Beatrice had found the conversation tiresome and was now skipping back and forth across the sidewalk. She collided with a stout gentleman and his hat fell off.

"Beatrice!" her mother called.

"Pick up my hat, little girl," the stout gentleman ordered. But the child shook her head and skipped away and he stooped with difficulty to pick it up himself.

"Brats!" he muttered. "Park's full of 'em."

"What a rude man!" Mrs. Westcott said indignantly. "I'm glad Beatrice didn't touch his hat."

Margaret rose and looked at her watch. "I ought to drop in at the gallery for a bit, and see how things are going."

"What gallery is it?" Mrs. Westcott asked.

"Pendlers," Margaret replied. "It's small but rather good."

"Oh, I know Pendlers," Mrs. Westcott said. "My husband bought a little painting there last year—a cottage set on a brown hill. He said it reminded him of something long ago—in his childhood, I think—and he hung it in his room."

Margaret's heart doubled its next beat. "It was mine," she said. "I painted the little cottage in which I live."

"Really?" Mrs. Westcott exclaimed. "I remember now that Bertram said I wouldn't know the painter. But it is a nice thing— and now I shall tell him I do know you."

Margaret mustered her pleasant smile. "Let me remain obscure," she said. She turned to the child. "Goodbye, Miss Beatrice."

The little girl skipped past, breathless. "I'm coming back—sometimes!" she called.

Margaret laughed into Mrs. Westcott's eyes and went away, holding her shoulders very straight and her head high.

Why should Bertram want a picture of the cottage? She walked quickly away from the park and toward the river. She knew where the Westcott house stood. On the day after his marriage she had read the account of the wedding. After the ceremony there had been a reception in the bride's home. The bride's father was dead and her mother lived in southern France and had come over only for the occasion. The house, so Margaret remembered, was a fairly new one, built only just before the father's death and remembered because it had made so exquisite a background for Sandra Westcott as a debutante.

She walked toward it, half-consciously, and approached it from a side street. She did not want to be seen, though there was slight chance of that. It was a high, narrow house of light gray stone. The doors and window frames and shutters were black. The gardens behind it faced the river, and through the high iron fence she could see a charming terrace and a pool. Then she heard a commotion, a child's laughter, a man's voice. A door opened and Bertram came out followed by Miss Beatrice, still in her blue frock and hat, as she had come from the park.

For one moment Margaret gazed at Bertram. He was listening to his daughter and laughing. The sun fell upon his black hair, his laughing face. Then she looked away, shocked at her own intrusion, and hastened from the spot. He looked completely happy. With a strange mingling of anger and relief she acknowledged this. Yet why had he bought the picture of the cottage? She had no place in this house. She did not want to think, when she went home again tonight, that in his private rooms there was a picture of something which reminded him of her. He had left her. Then let her be left.

She swung away from the river and held up her hand. A passing cab swerved toward her and stopped. "Pendler's Galleries," she said and gave the address. He had bought the painting just a year ago—perhaps on the anniversary of the day upon which they had decided, now so many years past, to take up their life together. Was it upon that day? And if so, what did he mean? Was he less happy than he looked?

A foreboding struck her. Her remittance from the gallery had been two hundred and fifty dollars more than she expected. She had accepted it, careless because Mr. Pendler had written that he had been able to get something more for one of the paintings. Two people wanted it and one of them had offered considerably more in order to get it. Ah, things were fitting into a strange pattern! She pressed her lips firmly together. Bertram must not think he could eat his cake and have it, too. What had happened was beyond change. He must stay by his own choice.

The cab slowed down and she pointed to the narrow entrance of the gallery squeezed between two taller houses. Then having paid her fare, she got out and went inside. Mr. Pendler was about to go out to lunch and she met him head on in the small square entry.

"I say!" he remonstrated. He was a small, round-faced, gray-haired man, never very successful because of his too kind heart, and yet somehow he managed always to hang on, from year to year. "You've winded me! I hope I didn't do anything to you."

"I'm sorry," she cried. "But I'm glad I've caught you in."

"I'm about to lunch," he said hesitantly. "I don't suppose you—"

She broke in, "No, thanks, and I won't keep you but a a minute. I want to ask you about my *Cottage on a Hillside*. You remember?"

They were in the gallery now. Her pictures looked nice. She was quite proud of them. There was something solid and real about them. Gazing at familiar landscapes, she felt a throb of homesickness. She must go home to-night—home to herself!

"Of course I remember," Mr. Pendler said in his mild tenor voice. "It was the one that I got such a good price for. There was an oldish woman wanted it—an Englishwoman—she said it reminded her of the Cotswolds. She was looking at it when a man came in, a dark fellow, and he took it away from her. 'I want this.' That's what he said. 'I beg your pardon,' she said, very stiff of course. 'I was about to buy it.' 'I'm sorry—but this happens to be a spot I know'—he said that in the most positive sort of voice. 'How much is it?' says she. I believe you'd put it at two hundred and fifty, hadn't you? Anyway, when I said that, the man simply said, 'I'll give you five hundred for it.'

"The Englishwoman was angry, of course, but I told her I had to think of your interests, and finally to placate her I told her you were quite dependent on your work. I'm afraid I made rather a sad case for you—that you didn't usually get high prices—not as high as you deserve—because of a somewhat—ah—conservative techniques and all that—you know, what I've said before. At any rate, the man got it. The Englishwoman never came back again, I'm sorry to say."

"I wish you hadn't said so much about me," Margaret said. Her face flushed.

Mr. Pendler pretended to be hurt. "Now, that's nice thanks for a good sale," he complained.

She tried to smile. "Of course I do thank you," she said.

Mr. Pendler looked at her somewhat fondly. "That's better. After all, you and I are old friends. How about lunch?"

"No, thanks," Margaret said firmly. "Please go on, I shall just sit here for a bit."

Mr. Pendler's avidity overcame his mild impulse. "Do," he said, "and if someone comes in, tell them you are the artist, and you'll find it's a wonderful help."

He bustled away and she was alone with her own pictures, except for a quiet mouse of a girl in the back, who was munching a sandwich while she copied figures into a ledger.

I won't have Bertram thinking about me, Margaret told herself. It will spoil everything.

What she meant was that it would make her sacrifice meaningless. She did not want him back, because with her he had been a lesser man than he could be. He could not make a great deal of money himself, nor could she, and he was not fitted for poverty. He was a plant that must live in the sun and their life together could provide only shadow.

She sat on the small, worn divan, facing her pictures, and one after the other they reminded her of her home, the bare round hill above the small lake, the big red barn of a neighbor farmer, the small grocery store interior, the Lutheran church, built high and narrow of red-brown stone, her own backyard and the chicken coop, the wooded glade of the stream. Here she could live, but Bertram could not.

I shall have to see him once more, simply to tell him— This, after half an hour, was her conclusion.

Yet how could she see him? It would be easy enough
to climb the marble steps in front of the great house and
ring the doorbell and ask for Mr. Westcott. But how absurd in the midst of such splendor to warn him against
the cottage!

And in a day or so, she knew, they were going to England. How absurd to meet him at all, perhaps! But
there was the picture of the cottage hanging on his walls,
where his eyes could fall upon it. And he had lied about
it to his wife. He had not said to her, straightly, "It is
where I lived for years with a woman I loved."

For he had loved her, and she did not doubt that in
some fashion he loved her still, even as she loved him.
She would never live with another man, though of her
own will she had set Bertram free and she did not want
him back. Yet at least he should not have lied. She hated
small lies and this one alarmed her. With her, too, Bertram had not had the courage to be entirely truthful. He
had owed money to another girl, when she first knew
that she loved him, and he had not had the courage to tell
her. The girl had come in anger to tell her own story.
That, too, was a day that could not be forgotten. They
had moved into the cottage only the week before, and it
was the first day on which Bertram had left her alone.
He had business, he said, at his publisher's office. In the
middle of the afternoon, when she had just looked at the
clock to see how many hours must pass before he came
back, she heard a footstep at the closed door, and thinking gladly that he had come home earlier than she had
expected, she had run to the door.

There upon the threshold she faced a tall, thin, dark-
eyed girl in whose face was a bitter beauty.

"Is this Bertram Westcott's house?" the girl had asked.

"Yes," Margaret had answered.

"I have come to collect a debt," the girl said. "We had

an apartment together and he left last week without pay-
ing his share of the rent."

For a long moment the two had looked at each other.
Then Margaret said, "He is not at home. I will pay you."

The girl had come in and sat down in silence while
Margaret found her purse and counted the bills.

"It's only right for you to pay my fare here and back to
New York," the girl said in her harsh young voice.
"After all, I've been put to expense."

Margaret looked at her steadily when she had counted
out the bills.

"You understand it is only the money I want," the girl
said.

"I do understand," Margaret replied.

The girl had gone after that, and Margaret had waited
for Bertram to come home. Why had he not told her?
But then she had not asked.

She did not ask when he came in, for he was depressed
that night. He said it was because he had not got the ad-
vance he wanted and he was short of money.

"I can't borrow from you," he had groaned, "and yet I
badly need twenty-five dollars."

"Never mind," she had said with terrible gentleness. "I
paid it for you."

And then she had told him, without accusation, exactly what had happened. He had listened and then he
had said, "Sorry," and he had moistened his lips.

"Never mind," she had said.

But she had minded profoundly, and it was the first
time that she knew there was something in him that was
not good. If he had had money, he would have paid his
debts, of course—he did not love money for its own sake.
But without money he was unstable.

Now, even with money, if he were not stable, then

indeed all their years were in vain. She decided suddenly
not to go home that night. She would stay one day
longer and devise some reasonable way of seeing him.

She felt tired suddenly and she went back to the hotel,
ate a late luncheon, and went to her room and slept for
two hours. When she woke it was evening. She rose and
went to a theater, came back and went to bed. And all
during these hours, waking and sleeping, the conviction
grew in her that she must see him and explain to him
that there was no return, for either of them. What had
been less than satisfying for him before had now become
impossible for her. In the night it dawned upon her that
there was still another reason—there was Miss Beatrice.

When she thought of the child she found that she had
fallen in love with her. In the darkness of her hotel room
she remembered the morning sunshine in the park, and
the way in which the little girl had danced, the way in
which she had lifted her dark eyelashes, had looked out
of her black eyes. She found that she remembered the set
of the fine head upon strong little shoulders, the small,
exquisite hands, and the black patent leather slippers.
She would go once more to the park and see this signifi-
cant, this wonderful child.

So in the morning she prepared to fulfill her desire.
She put on her heather-blue suit again and passing a
flowershop she bought a bouquet of small pink roses
which, she told herself, half laughing, she would present
to Miss Beatrice as a parting gift. She realized something
absurd in the fascination she felt for the child, but she
had always succumbed rather easily to exquisite children. Young Bertie's fat and surfeited countenance did
not yet attract her, and yet even he, a year or two hence
when he did not live for food alone, might prove fascinating, too. As for Miss Beatrice, never again, perhaps,

would she be at her present moment of perfection. Sophistication and small fears might later assail her. The world, even her world, might not be exactly her dream, but for the moment the dream still held.

So toward midmorning, fully determined that this was her last day, and that tonight, at some hour past midnight, she would be asleep in her own solitary bed, Margaret went again to the park.

This time the little knot of richly dressed children did not include Miss Beatrice or her mother or Bertie, neither the perambulator nor Nanny. Margaret sat down on her bench holding the little silver-paper box that concealed the pink rosebuds. The soft April day was suddenly clouded with her disappointment. She noticed for the first time that the sky, toward the sea, was filling with misty clouds, although the sun still shone here in the park. Perhaps, fearing rain, they had not come. Perhaps Miss Beatrice might even be ill, although yesterday she had looked in robust health.

She waited some fifteen minutes and then, sighing, she rose. It was at this moment that Miss Beatrice rounded the clump of shrubbery that hid the turn of the sidewalk. She was holding someone's hand, a man's, and Margaret instantly recognized Bertram. She sat down again, resisting her first impulse to escape.

"Here she is," Miss Beatrice sang. "Here's my Meggie—Meggie—"

She pulled her hand free and, skipping down the walk, she threw her arms around Margaret's neck. Margaret's arms enfolded her involuntarily, and she smelled the incomparable fragrance of a small girl's clean and scented flesh. Over her shoulder she looked up at Bertram, who now stood looking down at them both.

"I knew who this Meggie was," he said simply.

"I wanted to see you, too," Margaret said as simply. She loosened the small arms about her neck. . . . "That is, I want to talk with you about something."

He sat down beside her, and Miss Beatrice discovered the silver box.

"Is that for me?" she asked.

"It is," Margaret replied. "You may open it yourself."

They watched while the child pulled at the cord. "No—no—don't help—I can do it," she cried. When she saw the midget rosebuds a bright flush came over her cheeks. "Nobody gived me flowers for my own before," she said in a touching voice.

Margaret's eyes met Bertram's. "How could you not understand that she must have roses of her own?" she inquired, half-playfully.

"I never thought of it," he replied gravely.

Such enchantment was in the child's pleasure that strange tears came into Margaret's eyes.

Miss Beatrice lifted the little bouquet and looked at it. She buried her face in it and breathed in the fragrance. Then she looked up. "I just walk with my flowers in my hand, like this—" she said. She slipped from the bench and walked away, the roses in both hands at her breast.

"How absurd," Bertram said gazing after her. "She has everything, but only you discovered what she really wants."

"She didn't know she wanted them," Margaret said. "Nor did I, really. It is quite accidental that she's pleased. They make her feel important, perhaps—grown-up, like her mother."

Bertram did not answer. He glanced at her, and away again. "You're looking well," he said.

"So are you," Margaret said. "I never saw you look as you do now."

He was looking very handsome indeed. It was not only that his gray spring suit and topcoat were expensive and well tailored. His face looked honest and open. The old haggard, furtive expression was gone. He had grown a small, short moustache trimmed just above his finely shaped mouth. Even his mouth had changed. The droop was gone from his lips.

"Cigarette?"

"Yes, please."

She saw his hands, the skin smooth and clean, the nails tended. Their eyes met again and he did not look away.

"You really are happy," she announced, as though she was surprised.

"Terribly happy," he admitted.

"Then why did you come here this morning, Bertram?" she asked directly.

"Out of a sort of gratitude, I suppose," he replied. His eyes followed the figure of his daughter. She had turned and was coming toward them. But she did not stop. She was in a dream parade, herself and her roses.

"Gratitude?" Margaret asked.

"To you, to everything—" he replied. "That's why I came to thank you, Margaret, for all that you did for me."

"I never did anything for you," she murmured.

"You did," he insisted. "You made me go."

"But you wanted to go," she reminded him.

"I didn't altogether," he said. Then his face flushed and he looked at her. She saw shame in his eyes. "I want to tell you the truth," he said. "I know and you know that truth telling hasn't been—I haven't been able to rise to it always. But now somehow I can. When I married

Sandra—I wasn't really in love with her. She—was ready for me to be—in love with her. And I saw the chance to—to live as I've always wanted to live."

"Oh, Bertram!" Margaret's voice was a low cry of warning.

"No, wait—let me finish—I want you to know everything. It wasn't just greed. But I'd begun to know that I'd never be able to make the struggle. My books don't sell—not in the thousands I wanted them to. That is, alone, I'd never be really free of worry and maybe later even of debt. I'd begun to see that. So I thought, if I just had leisure, for one thing—not having to wonder whether I could keep my end up next year, and having time to do nothing but just think and dream up my best work. And suddenly I saw everything I'd wanted. And I felt I could really do my best work and be my best self—"

"You needn't tell me this," she said gently, "I know."

He gazed at her with new shame. "That's why you let me go?"

"Of course," she said in her most practical voice. "I can see for myself that it's a success. And if you can't love that pretty wife of yours, then you are a fool."

"I do love her," he said eagerly. "I began to love her almost at once. You see, Meg, with everything around me so beautiful, so much all I'd dreamed, it was simply inevitable that I turned to her, in a sort of gratitude to life."

"Of course," she agreed, "and so everything is right with you."

"Yes," he said. "And the strange thing is that loving her has put everything into perspective. I remember our years, Meg, yours and mine, with much tenderness. Your wonderful goodness—"

"They were good years," she said quietly, "but let's not talk about them. I'd rather know what you are going to do next—what you plan—"

His face changed. He looked resolute and eager. "I have a great scheme," he said. "Whether it works or not, I don't know. But Sandra wants me to try it. A good deal of her property is in the city and it's in rather miserable housing. She's a really good woman, Meg—you might think that her life would make her superficial and idle, but it doesn't. She wants the tenements rebuilt into good houses. I suppose I've helped her—you know how I was brought up. Anyway, we're going to England this summer to study housing with old Sir Robert Hiebens—he's done wonders there in the London suburbs." He turned to her again, and she could see there was no thought of her in his mind. "It's absolutely wonderful to be able to do great good things with one's life—"

"I can see that," she said, with complete understanding.

Miss Beatrice came past them again and Margaret called to her.

"My dear!"

Miss Beatrice stopped and looked at her with dreaming eyes.

"I must go," Margaret said. "Will you come and tell me goodbye?"

Miss Beatrice drew near in happy abstraction. She pointed at the bouquet. "I bit off some shut ones," she said. "I just want open ones."

"I hope you didn't swallow them," Margaret said.

"I 'pitted all them out," Miss Beatrice said. "On'y Bertie swallows down."

"Ah, you'll have to teach him better," Margaret said gravely. She stooped and kissed Miss Beatrice and then she turned to Bertram. "Goodbye," she said. "You've made me quite content."

He held her hand a minute. "And you are still there in the cottage?"

"Oh, yes. I shall be there the rest of my life."

She looked into his eyes for a moment, and did not see herself reflected there. But she saw him, assured at last.

"Goodbye," she said again, firmly.

"Goodbye, Meg."

She smiled at Miss Beatrice and walked away from them both without looking at them again. Now she really would catch the early train home. She looked at her wristwatch. She had an hour and it would be easy. She was longing to get back to her cottage. She quickened her footsteps. Then when she had rounded the turn of the road she stopped. She had said nothing at all to Bertram about the picture of the cottage on his walls! She had forgotten it. She stood a moment, smiling and shaking her head, unheeding of strangers who glanced at her with surprise as they passed her. Then she went on again, and peace was in her eyes.

The Woman in the Waves

THE SUN BEAT DOWN upon the sea. The man walking alone on the beach stared at the water, metallic blue except where yesterday's storm had left white breakers stretching far to the high horizon. Surely the horizon was higher than yesterday, the sea had swelled with the storm. It was impossible to work on such a morning but that was what his wife could never understand. She thought writing was as simple as plumbing. One should pick up his tools and begin. Maybe that had been the matter with the plumber, too, yesterday, that he could not begin, while she nagged him. The plumber had come because the cellar had overflowed so that the sump pump had stopped work.

"Hal, speak to him!" Kate had come into his room to make the demand.

"Leave the man alone, for God's sake," he had told her. "How can he work, either, with you coming to measure every five minutes what he's done?"

"Work?" Thus she had snorted. "Idling!"

That was yesterday. This morning, an hour ago, the door had opened and she looked in too brightly. He saw her, her auburn hair gorgeous, wiry and alive, her gray eyes magnificent. She was as beautiful as ever in his sight, but tense, too tense, too difficult to live with—though after yesterday she was trying to be good.

"Want anything before you start?" Her voice had been fearfully controlled. "I sharpened your pencils and I changed your typewriter ribbon."

He had exploded as he had sworn he would not. "For God's sake, just leave me alone!"

He was overdramatic again, as he had sworn, too, he would never be. Here on the beach he flung out his hands, palms upward, and then stared at them and let them drop. Hanging at his sides, they felt as useless as two empty bags and he lit a cigarette, trembling.

He had tried again while she stood straight and still in the doorway. "Look here, Kate, writing isn't just sitting down at a machine. There has to be time, empty time, for feeling and thinking. And I can't have you watching and waiting and secretly counting up pages at the end of the day."

She had stood motionless, except for the fire in the gray eyes. She had said in a dead, cold voice, "I haven't been able to pay bills for two months. We have no more credit. And my mother said she'd keep the children this summer so that you could be quiet and free, but that can't go on forever, either."

They were at it again.

"How can you talk to me like this in the morning, Kate? It kills the day. Fat chance now, at any work!"

"But what shall I do, Hal?"

He had lost all control, had shouted at her, hating himself. "Anything—anything, only leave me alone!"

Still she had refused to be angry. She stood, severe in her blue dress with its white collar and short sleeves. "I think you ought to get a job, Hal. A regular check every week, however small, would be something I could count on."

"Something you can count on!" he sneered. "You can't count on me, you mean!"

"No, Hal."

He was always helpless before her dreadful calm. "Then why don't you clear out? Leave me!"

"We have the children, Hal. They're too small for me to leave and go to work."

"Ah—" he had snarled at her, had jerked open the door, had rushed from the room out on the sands. The three-room cottage he had rented for the summer, cheaply enough, so that he could work, was barely a shelter. Each room opened to the outdoors and he had liked that and did like it now. It gave him escape. He strode across the sand and climbed the high dune to the left of the house. The wind was brisk and cool and the sun was hot. The narrow-bladed beach grass bent under the wind as though a vast hand smoothed it down. Up here on the dune was the bench he had made so that he and Kate could watch the moon rise, as indeed they often had. He loved her passionately and he knew it. If she left him he would really be finished, he supposed, the heart gone out of him. Then why did he long to be alone? It was the inexplicable division in him, that he could not part from her and yet he could not live with her. He had thought, when they left the children behind for the summer with her mother—the three small children all born too close together, because he and Kate were so crazy about each other—that at last he could work in peace. But there was no peace with her.

Staring down at the heavy wash of the breakers on the beach, he suddenly saw something brightly pink. The beach was wide and lonely, and no one was in sight. There was a cottage a half mile away, but that was all. The pink thing down there grew plain as the sea drained back. Then the breakers rushed in suddenly and covered it again, and he ran down the dune in time to be there when the wave crashed. The next wave was immense; it towered over him, curling its massed form. He saw the pink thing swept up into its greenish curve and he ran backward. He had come too close, the wave would break over him and he was no swimmer.

Crash and roar and the wave broke and threw the thing up on the beach, a pink dress of some sort, long dark hair—a woman! He raced down to snatch at the skirt, but the backwash was rolling her over and over into the sea and again he could not catch her. He had to run, because the wave was coming at him, gathering itself together like a tiger poised for a mouse, playing, he could swear it, with the woman.

He barely reached the dry sand, and as though to tease him with terror the wave raced beyond him. He felt the icy water swirling about his ankles, pulling him down. He stumbled and fell on all fours and crawled away, yelling aloud.

But the wave which had tried to pounce on him had washed the inert woman high up the beach. He caught her skirt this time with a firm grip. The wet stuff held, it was strong, and he jerked and pulled and dragged her out of the grasp of the next wave. Then he sat down, panting and exhausted with terror. He was safe, he was alive, but here was this woman. Dead! There could be no doubt of it. He stared down at her as she lay a few feet from where he sat on a blackened spar from some ship burned at sea. She lay all straightened by the water, her hair black and smooth, her face drained pale, and her arms stiff and white. Her hands were like sea creatures, outspread and delicate. Her feet were bare and her dress had been torn from her shoulders. She was young, almost a child, or perhaps the water had washed all expression from her face. Her eyes were closed and sunken, and her mouth, slightly open, showed small white teeth, very perfect.

He got to his feet, forgetting everything but the way she looked, and the sun beat down upon them hotly. Where had she come from? She wore a dress of some strangely heavy material, not silk, something strong and almost coarse, but closely woven. It was girdled tightly about her little waist. She had not been in the water long, her flesh was still whole and clean, except that some sea creature had nibbled at her right foot and the wound had bled. But the water had washed that clean, too. He wondered whether he should try artificial respiration and knew it was no use. She was stiffened in death. She had been dead several hours, he guessed. She must have drowned some time last night. Perhaps she had been dancing, down the beach where there were dance halls, three or four miles away, a horrible place where raucous amusements and cheap shops lured the children of city workers who did not know what to do with themselves on a vacation. But she did not look like any of them. Her little feet were fine. Perhaps she had been dancing on a yacht, yet hardly in such rough weather would a yacht have been out on the sea, unless it had been caught by the storm. The storm had risen suddenly in the Caribbean and had swept up the coastline, skipping in its haste the curves and indentations of harbors and coves. Only the monstrous surf had told of the storm. But on a yacht would she not have worn some sort of jewelry? There was not even a ring on her hands. Perhaps she had worn beautiful jewelry and it had been robbed. She might have gone out for a moment alone on a deck or a pier. Perhaps there had been a quarrel with her lover and she had rushed outdoors, simply to be away from him. She had a proud, stern, little face. The lips were white, but the eyelashes on her cheeks were dense and black. A quarrel, perhaps, in which it had been the man who had quarreled with her, a jealous lover who in the darkness of night had thrown her to the sea rather than think of losing her to another.

A harsh voice broke across him like a whip. "Look here, man, what's this?" He looked up, bewildered, and got to his feet stumbling. He had forgotten everything except the story he was making.

"I don't know—this woman was washed in just now."

The man was huge, a prizefighter of a man, naked except for close black trunks about his narrow hips. He had been swimming and the water glistened on his wet brown flesh and thick, oil black hair.

"And you stand there!" he shouted. "Why don't you get the Coast Guard, or the police?"

"What can anybody do now?" Hal asked and was surprised at the sadness of his voice.

The man looked suspicious. "Look here, you do know something about this?"

"I don't—only what I've said. I climbed that dune this morning—live in that cottage—and I looked down and saw her pink dress. I ran down and tried to pull her out. It took me several minutes because the waves kept drawing her back. The undertow must be frightful after the storm."

The more he talked, the more suspicious the man was, he could see. He was a simple fellow, easily suspicious, as the simple-minded are.

"We've got to find somebody," he muttered.

They looked up and down the beach. There was nobody.

"We could walk up to that other cottage," Hal suggested.

"Who lives in it?" the man asked. "I'm only a weekender."

"I don't know them—a young couple honeymooning, I heard."

"Didn't you ever see them?"

"I saw her at a distance, not near. I did see him close one day but we didn't speak."

"Funny on a beach like this that you didn't get friendly."

"Oh well, they were honeymooning, and I'm a writer—supposed to be working."

The man looked at him, suspicious again. A writer!

"Think we ought to leave her by herself while we go after somebody?"

"You can stay, if you like," Hal said.

"No, thanks," the man said hastily. "It wasn't me that found her."

"I could get my wife," Hal said, hesitating.

The man welcomed this. "Why don't you?"

"I can call her from the dune."

"All right."

He ran to the top of the dune and called, making a megaphone of his hands.

"Kate! Oh-h-h Kate!"

She came out broom in hand and waved.

"Come quickly, Kate!"

She put down the broom and walked as swiftly as the sand would let her.

"Kate"—he was all breathless—"Kate, a woman has been washed up. I was standing here just like this when I saw her pink dress down there."

She was at his side now. "Who's that man?"

"He just came by. We have to find somebody. He doesn't want to stay with the woman by himself."

"You mean you want me to stay with a strange man and a dead woman?"

She was unwilling, he could see. "I'll stay and you go."

"I won't go with him alone."

"Take your choice then."

"I'll stay with her, and you take him. How do we know who he is? Why should he just happen along?"

"Oh, Kate, don't ask questions—I don't know anything, but we've got to find someone, I tell you."

He seized her hand and they ran down the dune. The man was standing with his back to the dead woman, staring out to sea.

"That's rough water," he said, turning.

"My wife," Hal said.

The man nodded without telling his name.

"She says she'll stay," Hal said.

"Then let's get going," the man said, "though I don't know why I mix myself up in this. I'm not looking for trouble."

"Neither am I," Hal said.

He hesitated. "Sure you'll be all right, Kate?"

She glanced at the woman and away again. "Yes, I'll be all right, but come back quickly."

The two men walked away then down the beach to the lonely cottage. Ten minutes and they were there. Hal stepped upon the small porch and knocked at the closed door. There was no answer and he knocked again. A window was open and a white curtain fluttered. Once more he knocked, and still there was no answer.

"Looks like nobody's home."

"Open the door," the man said.

Hal opened the door slowly, reluctantly. What if they were asleep inside? You could never tell about honeymooners. But no one was there. The bare little room was clean except for a sift of sand that had heaped inside the open window. Two chairs and a table, bunks, a stove and some driftwood piled beside it, and that was all.

"They've gone," Hal said stupidly.

The man could not believe it, but it was so. There was no sign of life.

Wait, there was a scrap of paper, half hidden under the stove to Mr. and Mrs. Jim Bradley, Seacove, New Jersey, and somebody had written in pencil on the back, a grocery list, apparently, with the prices quoted down, of eggs, bread, butter, dried beef, oranges. The handwriting was very young, almost childish. "This don't seem to tell much," the man said.

Hal took the envelope from his hand. "Maybe the postmark—"

The postmark was surprisingly clear. Freedom Hollow, Maryland. He remembered the place. He had driven through it once when he was going on a fishing trip to Onancook on Chesapeake Bay, a cluster of wooden houses, as he remembered, insignificant except that one of them had unusually beautiful ironwork on the porch, as beautiful as any he had ever seen in New Orleans. But it had been only an orphanage, though once the house of a rich man, a retired sea captain.

"Let's take this anyway," he said.

"We ought to get back and report to the police," the man said.

When they got back Kate was sitting beside the dead woman, fanning her. It made a strange sight at a distance, almost as though the woman were alive.

"She can't have come to," the man muttered.

Hal did not answer. He broke into a run and Kate turned her head. "You were a long time," she said reproachfully. "It's been burning hot—and the flies!" The biting small black flies that looked as innocent as house flies and were actually instruments of torture were everywhere. She was fighting them off herself as well as from the dead woman.

"What are we going to do?" she asked helplessly when she heard Hal's report.

"Get the police," he said. "Maybe we should have done that in the first place."

"I can't sit out here any longer," Kate said. She got to her feet and slapped her bare arms and neck. The flies swarmed down upon the woman. "I can't stand that either," she cried. "You'll have to carry her into the house."

"We dassent disturb a corpse," the man said.

"She's already been disturbed," Kate said. "She was in the ocean and Hal pulled her out."

The man hesitated, but it was clear in a moment that Kate was right. The woman could not be left and nobody could stay with her.

Hal stooped. "I'll take her head and shoulders," he said to the man. "You take her feet."

They marched heavily over the sand, carrying their burden, and Kate followed behind. They carried the woman through the door Kate had left open.

"Put her in the end room," Kate said. "Then hurry." There was a cot in the end room and the men laid her there and then walked up the beach toward the town, side by side.

"Well," the man said when they got there, "I guess you won't need me anymore. I'll go my way."

Hal hesitated. "I might need you as a witness. What if they ask how I got her into the house?"

The man looked stubborn. "I had nothing to do with it—just happened to pass by."

"That's all I did, too," Hal retorted. "I just happened to see her in the water."

"You pulled her out, though," the man said.

"Who wouldn't have done that?" Hal said with some heat. "You would have, too. It's all been chance."

"Okay, okay, don't get mad at me," the man said. "I'm staying at the Eagle Hotel. You can find me if you need me. I'll be here until tomorrow night."

"But your name?"

"Oh, that's right—we haven't been introduced, have we—queer, too, after all this! I'm Joe Miller."

"Thanks," Hal said.

They parted, and he went to the police station. Now that he was alone he felt nervous. It was strange to walk into the station and say that he had pulled a dead woman out of the water and that she lay in the extra bed in his cottage. Yet that was what had happened.

Inside the station a stout man sat with his coat off, eating a ham sandwich.

"Come in," he grunted. "Sit down. Hot as blazes, ain't it?"

"Yes," Hal said. He sat down, "I have to report a woman washed up on the beach."

"What's that?" The fat man put down the sandwich and stopped chewing, his cheeks bulging.

Hal told the story quickly.

The fat man began chewing again. "You say you never saw the woman before?"

"No. There was a young couple just up the beach, and I thought it might be the woman there." He told the man about the empty cottage.

"Wasn't it?"

"I don't know—here's an envelope I found."

The fat man took it gingerly and stared at it. "Why, I know this here feller! They come by last night, him and his wife, said they was going home on account of his mother being sick. I reckon it isn't them—though the girl was crying."

"I don't know," Hal said patiently. "I just want to get somebody on the job, the coroner, an undertaker, to remove the body. My wife is alone there. I wish you'd take over."

The man gulped down his sandwich and rose. "Sure," he said heartily. "I'll get right on the job."

"I'll be waiting," Hal said.

It was strangely quiet in the cottage when he got back. He found Kate sitting in the old rocking chair, doing nothing. That in itself was queer. She was so possessed with restlessness these days, so compelled by anxiety, that he had feared to find her frantic. Instead, she sat rocking to and fro, her face composed, her eyes remote.

"Hello, darling," he said. "I found the local policeman. He'll take care of things."

He bent to kiss her and she clung to him for an instant. He sat down on the step in the doorway.

"Sorry I couldn't get back sooner," he went on.

"You haven't eaten," she said.

"I can't just yet."

"I can't either. Everything is ready in the oven, though."

"Let's wait until they've all gone."

"I'd like to walk on the beach except that I don't think we should leave her."

"No, I suppose not."

She rocked back and forth slowly and he gazed out over the sea. The wind had gone down, the sky was clear and the sea blue. The waves were quieting, now that they had done their worst. It was wonderful to be still— no roar of the surf, no words of anger. He sat motionless and thoughtful.

After a time she spoke. "I keep wondering about her. I think she killed herself, Hal."

"What makes you think that?" he demanded, curious.

"I wasn't going to tell you," she said irrelevantly. "I was just going to do it. I've been feeling for a long time that I had to. I thought I was doing you no good, and yet I couldn't help myself. I should never have been your wife, Hal."

"Oh, come now, Kate." He was alarmed and irritated again. She was nervous, after all.

"I'm not upset," she said calmly. "That's what you're thinking, isn't it?"

"Of course you're upset," he declared.

"I was going to walk down to the beach tonight," she said. "I tried to go last night, but the waves were so big I couldn't face them. But tonight it would be still, I thought. I was going to walk out into the water when it was dark, and tomorrow morning you would wonder where I was—I wouldn't leave a letter, for that is cruel. Why, if one decides to die, should there be a letter? It is all finished, there is nothing more to say. You might wonder where I was, but the sea would answer that. The sea always gives back what it takes, doesn't it? So there I'd be, I thought, washed clean and cold, and nothing would matter anymore. I wouldn't be able to scold or nag—and the children could stay with my mother, and you could work."

He was horrified. She was in earnest, she had actually been planning this outrage!

"It is so strange," she mused before he could speak, "so strange that she should do it last night instead of me. I wonder that the great waves didn't frighten her. She must have been brave, much braver than I am. If I were brave, I suppose I wouldn't worry about the bills."

"Kate, will you stop!" he cried.

She looked at him, her gray eyes kind and soft, and she stopped. But she got up and went into the other room, the room where the dead woman lay, and it was a long time before he could follow her, an hour perhaps, and he could not have followed her then except that the policeman, not in his uniform and sweating hot, came rumbling up the sands in an old car with soft tires. He had two other men with him and the pallid plump man could not be anyone but the undertaker.

"We got here finally," the fat man panted. "It took me time to round up everybody, coroner and all. We're all here now. Where's the body?"

"Just a moment," Hal said. "My wife's in there."

He had to go in, and he opened the door. Kate was kneeling by the bare cot where the dead woman lay. "I've brushed her hair," she said, "and I have dried her dress as much as I could. I put stockings on her feet to hide that hurt place. She's so pretty, even now."

"You'd better come away," he said. "They're here."

She came obediently, and stayed away while he gave his story to the coroner.

"Any witnesses to all this?" the coroner asked. He was a small thin man, with alert blue eyes.

Hal hesitated and then he gave the name of the man in the Eagle Hotel. "He was simply passing by, though," he added.

"That's all right," the man said. "He's a witness, just the same."

It was soon told, the men listening soberly. "We'll take her away now," the undertaker said.

"We ought to wait a few days before she's buried," the policeman said. "She must have folks."

"There'll have to be an autopsy," the coroner said.

"Maybe she didn't drown. Lots of foul play on the shore, you know. The sea seems easy, but it ain't. It always tells the story in its own way."

"My wife and I will walk on the sands while you finish here," Hal said.

He took Kate's hand and they walked away, down to the now harmless waves.

"I shall never cease to wonder what made her do it," Kate began.

He interrupted her, unable to hear what she might say again about herself.

"You heard the coroner say it might be foul play."

Kate shook her head at this, her auburn hair stirring about her face. "I think she did it. I think she was terribly sad and terribly brave. That's dangerous when it's all bottled up in a woman." She waited and then she said slowly, as if she were in pain, "I know because I felt that way, too."

"Kate," he cried, "why didn't you tell me this before?"

She looked at him with a frightening humility in her stone gray eyes. "I didn't want to intrude. I wanted to leave you free even from me. I just wanted enough money to pay the bills, that's all, because people get so angry when we owe them money. When they're angry I can't go back to them. But where will I buy bread and milk and the meat for the children? I did make a garden for vegetables, but what about the rest?"

"Oh, Kate," he cried. "Oh, Kate, my wife!"

He sank his head in his hands and she crouched on the hot sand beside him and wept.

So near had he been to tragedy, and it might have been her dress that he saw in the waves, this blue gingham dress that she wore every day for her work! It might have been so, for he had divined that she held in her somewhere from her childhood the power for despair, a childish despair that might shrink, as she had said, from the crashing waves, but that could possess her nevertheless and make it quite possible and even pleasing to her to walk quietly into a smooth sea until it covered her up. He had divined it, but he had refused to know it until now she herself told him.

He gathered her roughly into his right arm against him. "Don't you know I love you?"

"Oh, yes," she said, "I know that, but I know love isn't enough for you. I knew that long ago."

He was silent, aghast that this was true. For a man like him love wasn't enough.

"Yet I must have it," he insisted. "Life wouldn't be complete without it."

"I know that, too," she said. "But it wouldn't have to be me. If it's only love you need, there would be other women who could give it to you. For me it isn't love that is important. It's you. And when I felt I was no use to you—well!" She threw out her small square hands in a young and helpless gesture.

He could not answer because he was ashamed. For instead of thinking only of her at this moment there was welling up in him a familiar and intoxicating emotion. He recognized it and his heart was instantly washed clean of fear and sorrow. He felt himself potent with creation. The sudden reality of life, crystallized clear into this moment, impelled him with inspiration. He had touched the source again. Oh, he would lose it, he fumbled and halted when he lost the touch, but today he had it.

"I have my story," he cried.

"What is it?" she asked, her eyes wide.

"It will begin with the woman washed up from the sea."

"But you don't know her—"

"I do know her," he insisted. "I know why she threw herself into the water last night. It was because something she had dreamed of all her life didn't come true at the appointed hour. A dream has to come true at the appointed hour, because if it doesn't it will never be the same."

She said in wonder, "Oh, Hal, never listen to me again! I don't care about the check coming in every week if I can see you look like this!"

He stood up and drew her strongly with him. "Why do you say that it isn't you that matters?" he demanded. "No one else in the world could understand me except you."

Nevertheless, days later, she concealed her surprise that the end of the story was really almost as he had written it. "Don't you want to wait?" she had asked. "Don't you want to find out exactly how it was? They'll soon know, I suppose."

"No," he had said. "I've already made the end of the story. It was the honeymoon couple, of course. Did you ever see the man's face? Handsome as a god, as they say—and that means blind as a god and stupid as a god, knowing nothing beyond himself. That is what she discovered in the night. It doesn't matter how many nights it really was—she discovered it in the night. But she was a religious little soul—did I tell you she had run away to marry him? That was the way it was, and so she had nothing at all except him? She had killed her soul for him, and renounced heaven. So there was literally no place for her to go, except out into the sea."

"Oh, Hal," she cried, "you have read the newspaper, after all!"

"I swear I haven't," he said, for he had not.

"But look!" she cried. She thrust at him the day's

newspaper and the story was there, almost as he had told it. There were details he had not written, that the dead woman was an orphan child, that she had never known parents or family, that she had simply stepped from the orphanage into marriage. The man had been a truck driver who delivered food at the kitchen door, and she had been put to help in the kitchen. These were the details that made the story small and plain, but he had not needed them. His imagination had seen her through Kate, his own wife, and he had made her woman and the truck driver man, and that was perhaps what they really were.

Whatever his magic was, he had unwillingly cast its spell over Kate. She had never quite believed in him but now she did. She had never wholly understood what he was and now she did.

When she read what he had written she clenched her teeth to think how she had all but destroyed him. Love? Any woman could love a man—it was all too easy indeed to love him, but faith was what he needed to live. Faith was the bread of life, and she alone could make it.

She did not want to weep again. She was not a weeping woman, and he knew it and weeping would alarm him. Instead, she spoke in an ordinary voice, "Now I see what you can do, Hal, I shall never doubt you again. I shan't ask you to forgive me, that would be silly. Instead—count on my eternal faith, will you?"

"Yes," he said. They exchanged a long, strong look and she tossed the newspaper into the wastebasket.

Secrets of the Heart

Mrs. Allenby listened to her daughter's plans for the holiday, and then it was time for her to make her announcement. "I won't be here for Christmas," Mrs. Allenby said, keeping her voice as casual as she could.

Her daughter Margaret stared at her. "What *do* you mean?" Margaret demanded. "It's impossible! Not here for Christmas? Where are you going?"

"I haven't decided," Mrs. Allenby said. She carefully tied a silver bow on a small package. Inside was a brooch for Margaret, a circle of pearls set in gold that she had found only yesterday in an antique shop. When the package was tied to her satisfaction she handed it to her daughter.

"For you—not to be opened until. . . . I'll deliver the other gifts for all of you, parents and children, to each of your houses before I go."

Margaret, about to leave after an hour of lively talk, sat down again in the blue velvet chair by the fire. They were in her mother's living room. The December sun was blazing through the windows, paling the flames that were crackling in the low grate.

"But, Mother, you've never been away at Christmas-time!" Margaret cried.

"So this year I shall be," Mrs. Allenby said, her voice pleasant but firm.

She leaned back in her own blue velvet chair opposite and gazed at her daughter affectionately. "You're putting on a little weight, aren't you, dear?"

"Don't try to change the subject," Margaret said. "No, I'm not putting on weight and I'm *not* pregnant, if that's what you mean. Four children are enough—though I'd rather enjoy a baby again! Benjie will be starting school next year and the house will be empty. But back to you now—when are you going?"

"I haven't decided," Mrs. Allenby said. "Perhaps tomorrow but perhaps not until Christmas Eve. I'll see when I get ready."

"I shan't enjoy Christmas, at all," Margaret said rather shortly.

"You will," Mrs. Allenby said. "And I suggest that you take the opportunity of my absence and not have the other families with you. Four of you, with your accumulated children, adorable as they are—well, it's simply too much, even of those adorable grandchildren."

"Mother, if I didn't know you love us—"

Mrs. Allenby interrupted. "Indeed, I love you all, but I think you should be alone for Christmas, each pair of parents with their own children, the children alone with only their own parents and brothers and sisters. You've no idea—" She stopped.

"Idea of what?" Margaret demanded, her eyes very blue under her dark hair. She was a small creature, but possessed of a mighty spirit. Hot or cold, she was all extremes.

"How peaceful it would be," Mrs. Allenby said rather lamely.

Her daughter looked at her critically. "You aren't being noble or something, are you? Thinking we don't want you or something stupid like that?"

"Oh no, indeed," Mrs. Allenby said. "Nothing like that."

Margaret was silent for a full half-minute, regarding her mother with suspicious eyes. "You aren't carrying on some sort of secret romance?"

Mrs. Allenby blushed. "Margaret, how *can* you—"

"You *are!*" Margaret cried.

"I am *not*," Mrs. Allenby said flatly. "At my age," she added.

"You're still pretty," Margaret said.

"Oh, nonsense," Mrs. Allenby said.

Margaret looked at her mother fondly and then rose. "Well, keep your secrets, but I still tell you I shan't enjoy Christmas for a minute, wondering where you are." She put her arms about her mother and kissed her. "And this present—the package is so small I know it's expensive and you shouldn't have. . . ."

"It's my money, darling," Mrs. Allenby said, laughing.

Margaret kissed her mother again, ran to the door and stopped to look back. "Tell me where you're going," she asked again, her voice coaxing.

Mrs. Allenby laughed. "Go home and tend your children," she said gaily and waved goodbye.

Alone with the fire, the winter sun streaming across the Aubusson carpet, the bowl of holly on the table, the book-lined walls, Mrs. Allenby was suddenly aware of a deep relief. She loved her house, she loved her children and their children, but—but what? She did not know what came after this *but*. Simply that she longed not to be here on Christmas. She would leave early in the morning of Christmas Eve. That would see her at the cabin in Vermont by nightfall. Now she rose, gathered some bits of silver cord and wrapping paper which she threw into the fire, and went upstairs to pack.

By eight the morning of Christmas Eve she was in her car and headed north. Snow threatened from a smooth gray sky, and in Vermont, the radio told her, it was already snowing. They had often gone skiing in Vermont in the old days, she and Leonard, before they were married. And it was to Vermont that they had gone for their honeymoon, but in October, and too early for skiing. How glorious it had been, nevertheless, the mountains glittering in scarlet and gold!

"In celebration of our wedding," Leonard had said.

It was because of him, of course, that she wanted to have Christmas alone, and in Vermont. They had always come here alone. It had been his demand.

"Let's never go to Vermont with the children—always alone," he had said.

"Selfish, aren't you," she had teased, with love.

"Plenty of other places to ski with them," he had retorted.

"Of course we mustn't let them know—they'd be hurt," she had said.

"No reason why they should know this place even exists," he had agreed.

That was just after they had built the cabin and now it was the place essential to her, for there she could refresh, revitalize, her memory of Leonard. She was frightened because she was forgetting him, losing him—not the sum total of him, of course, but the clarity of detail of his looks, the dark eyes and the sandy hair. He had died so heartbreakingly young, the children still small, and their own children never to see their grandfather—see the way he walked, his tall spare frame moving in his own half-awkward, curiously graceful fashion. The memory came strong at Christmas, especially—he had loved sprawling on the floor with his children, showing them how to play with the toys he chose for them with such care.

The snow was beginning to fall now, a few flakes, growing heavier as she drove out of the traffic and toward the mountains. She would reach the cabin this evening late. Leonard had designed the cabin before any of the children were born so it had only three rooms. He had not wanted children too soon.

"Let's be solid with each other first," he had said.

They had come to the cabin often during the first years of their life together, as often as he could get away from the laboratories where he worked as a research scientist. After the children came, it was less often and at last, when he was dead, not at all—that is, she had never come back alone. Yet she had not thought of selling it. Gradually she had not thought of it at all, though she knew now she had not forgotten it.

The hours sped past. She was a fast driver but steady, Leonard always said, and it was she who usually did the driving when they went to the cabin, the quiet hours giving him time to think. He had said gratefully, "What it means to a man like me not to have to talk—"

Yet, some laboratory problem solved, he would be suddenly gay with lively talk. They had good talk together, and it was not until his voice was stilled in death that she realized how good the talk was, and that there always had been something to talk about.

The day slipped past noon, and the snow continued to fall. Before darkness fell she reached the village and there she stopped to buy food for a day or two. The old storekeeper was gone, and a young man, a stranger, had taken his place. He looked at her curiously but asked no questions as he carried the box of groceries to her car. She drove on then in the dusk, up the winding graveled road to the top of the snow-covered hill. The road narrowed, and within a few yards she saw the cabin. The trees had grown enormous, but the cabin was still there, as enduring as Leonard had planned it to be.

She got out of the car and lifted a flat stone. Yes, the key was still there, too, the big brass key.

"I hate little keys," Leonard had said. "They lose themselves on purpose."

So they had found the huge, old brass lock, a heavy and substantial one. She fitted the key into the hole, and the door creaked open. Dear God, it couldn't be the same after all these years—but it was the same.

"We must always leave it as though we were coming back tomorrow," Leonard had said.

It was dusty, of course, and it smelled of the forest and dead leaves. But it had been built so solidly that bird and beast had found no entrance. The logs in the great fireplace were ready to light, and in the bedroom the bed was made—damp and musty, doubtless, but there it was, and the fire would soon drive out the dampness. She would hang the bedclothes before the chimney piece.

She lit the fire and the big oil lamp, then she unpacked the car, and sat down in the old rocking chair to rest a few minutes before preparing food. So here she was, unexpectedly really, for she had made no long-standing plans to come here. It had come over her suddenly, the need to find Leonard somehow, even to remember him, and this had happened when she was buying the brooch for Margaret. It had taken a little time to find it.

"Are you looking for something for yourself?" the young woman in the antique shop had asked.

"No," she had replied, "I'm just looking."

"A tie pin for your husband, perhaps?" the young woman had persisted.

"I have no husband," she had replied, shortly. Then she had corrected herself. "I mean—he died many years ago."

But her instinctive reply had frightened her. No husband—was she forgetting Leonard? Impossible—but perhaps true? And here it was Christmas again, and if ever he was not to be forgotten it was at Christmas, the time he loved best. And suddenly all her heart had cried out for him. Yet where was he to be found, if not in memory? And suddenly she needed to be alone this Christmas. The children, grown into men and women, and their children, whom he had never seen, were strangers to him, and living in their midst, she had almost allowed herself to become a stranger to him, too.

She got up to open a can of soup and put it on the stove. Then she found the dustcloths in a drawer where she had folded them, freshly washed, and she dusted the furniture before she ate. The fire was roaring up the chimney and the room had lost its chill. The snow was falling more heavily now and by morning it would be piled against the door. The main road would be plowed, however, since there were many new houses for skiers who had started coming here in increasing numbers—she had read of that. And Leonard always saw to it that the snow shovel hung inside the shed at the end of the cabin.

She pulled the small drop-leaf table before the fire and set out her supper, a bowl of bean soup, bread and cheese and fruit, and she ate with appetite. When she had eaten she folded the table away against the wall. Then she heated water and took her bath in a primitive tin tub. It was all so easy, so natural, to do what they had done, she and Leonard, here alone in the forest. Clean and warm in her flannel nightgown, she went into the bed, now warm and dry, but still smelling of autumn leaves, and fell into dreamless sleep.

She woke the next morning to sunshine glittering upon new-fallen snow. For a moment she did not know where she was. Here, where she had always been with Leonard, her right hand reached for him instinctively. Then she remembered. It was Christmas Day and she was alone. No, not alone, for her first thought summoned Leonard to her mind. She lay for a moment in the warm bed. Then she spoke.

"I can talk out loud here—there is no one to hear me and wonder."

She heard her own voice and was comforted by its calm. "I can talk all I want to out loud," she went on.

A pleasant peace crept into her heart and body, as gentle as a perfume, and she smiled.

"We spent our first Christmas here," she reminded herself.

They had driven up through snow flurries that year, and, as she had done, only together, they had waked to another day of sun upon snow. Then Leonard had got up to light the fire and heat the water.

"Lie still, sweetheart," he had commanded. "There's no one here to hurry us—a glorious Christmas Day."

He had come back to bed, shivering, and they had begun the day with love.

Later they had breakfasted on the small table before the fire, and while she washed the dishes, he had gone out and cut a little tree and had brought it in, glistening with ice, and they had decorated it. They had remembered to bring tinsel and a few silver ornaments, and they had tied their gifts to the branches.

"I've planned every moment of this day," he had said. When they had admired the tree, they opened their presents. She had given him a gold band for his wrist-watch and he had given her a necklace that was a delicate silver chain.

"To bind you to me forever," he had said, slipping it over her head.

She had loved the chain through all the years and wore it often. She had even brought it with her, to wear with her red wool dress today. Remembering, she got up from bed and ran into the other room to build the fire.

She laid bits of bark and slivers of dry wood on the lingering coals. She had made such a mighty fire last night that under the ashes there were still live coals. In a few minutes the blaze sprang up in sharp flickering points. Leonard had taught her how to make a proper fire that first year, and she had never forgotten.

She filled the big kettle now with water from the kitchen pump and hung it on the crane above the fire. When the water was hot she washed and dressed, putting on her red dress, and sat down at the table for breakfast. And when she finished eating and washed the dishes, she put on Leonard's lumber jacket, which hung as usual behind the door, and went out to cut a tree—a very tiny one, just to set on the table. The tree ornaments were where Leonard had put them, years ago, in the wall drawer under the window and she tied them on the tree. Then she found the gift she brought for herself in her bag, and she tied it to the tree.

"A year or two and perhaps there'll be more than the two of us," Leonard had said, on their third Christmas. "We've had over two years alone. Now let's have our children—four of them—close together while we're still young. They can enjoy each other and us, and there'll be years for us alone after they've grown up and don't need us anymore."

"We can't bring a baby to this cabin in the middle of winter," she had said.

"We'll take Christmas where we find it," he had told her.

And sharing his desire, as she loved to do because she loved him, by the next Christmas they had a son, named for his father but called Lennie. He was three months old that Christmas and they spent it, the three of them, in their first house, a modest one on a quiet street in the small Connecticut town where she still lived.

"I'm sure he sees the tree," Leonard had insisted.

Lennie, lying on the rug, had stared steadily at the glittering tree, still not a very big tree but one loaded with gifts. Then he had smiled, and both she and Leonard had laughed and reached for each other's hand.

"I'm glad we're alone, the three of us," Leonard had said. "It's selfish of me not to want to go to either of our parents, but we have our own home now, you and I and our child. That's the trinity of life, my love."

In less than two years they had their daughter, Margaret.

"Another one and we'll need a bigger house," Leonard had said on Christmas Day.

Lennie, an accomplished walker by then, had been pulling things off the tree. Margaret had been propped on pillows on the couch.

"Oh, Leonard, the payments on this one—" she had cried.

Before she could finish he had stopped her with a kiss. "A present for you, darling—I'm being promoted."

She had reproached him in her joy. "And you didn't tell me!"

"Christmas gift," he had said.

They had started to build their new house that next spring. By November it was still not quite finished but they moved in anyway to celebrate Dickie's birth.

"It was such an occasion," she said aloud now, smiling.

She noticed then that the fire was burning low, the logs mere coals and the ashes falling. She rose and got a new log from the stack, though it took all her strength to lift it.

"I wish you would realize you aren't a giant," Leonard had said so many times. "You're too impulsive—you see something you want done and you rush to do it yourself, forgetting that you have an able-bodied man around."

The log fell crookedly and she had to kneel to straighten it. Flames sprang from the coals and she dusted her hands and sat down again in the rocking chair.

That first Christmas in their new house had been a blessed one. Two little children ran about the room, shouting with delight, and Dickie sat propped on the couch. Lennie had his first tricycle and Margaret her first real doll. She loved dolls from that day on, and from them learned to love babies—nowadays her own. But little Dickie. . . .

The tears were hot against her eyelids now and she bit her lip. There was more than joy to remember. There was also sorrow. Dickie had died before the next Christmas. Death had come suddenly, stealing into the house. She had put him to bed one night, a few days before Christmas, and in the morning had gone to wake him and had found him dead. The beautiful little body was there, white as the snow outside the window, and the blue eyes were still closed as it in sleep. Unpredicted, unexplained, and she still wept when she thought of it. She wept now as if she had lost him only yesterday. Back then she had known she must try to comfort Leonard, although in weeks upon weeks, he would not be comforted. But for his sake she had been compelled not to weep, compelled to seem brave when she was not brave.

"Don't even speak of Christmas," he had said that dreadful year. And against every beat of her own aching heart she had persuaded him.

"Dearest, there are the others. They've been looking forward to Christmas Day. We must go on as usual—as best we can."

"You are right, I know," he had said at last. "But don't expect too much of me."

They had both been glad when Christmas Day was over, that heartbreaking day.

"Oh, how did we ever, . . ." she whispered now and sobbed.

It was still unendurable and she got up from the rocking chair.

"I shall make myself a cup of tea," she said aloud.

While the tea was steeping, she made herself a turkey sandwich from the sliced meat she had bought the day before. The sun was already past zenith and the room had lost its glow. When she had eaten the sandwich and had drunk her tea she felt better. She put another log on the fire and then she went to the window seat and sat looking out on the wintry landscape, the field covered with snow, the spruce forest tipped with snow, the white birch trees, and the peak of the mountain beyond, all drenched in the pure light of afternoon.

She and Leonard had endured that terrible Christmas, and in the spring she was pregnant again.

By the next Christmas Day, Ronald was born and two years later Ellen.

"Enough," Leonard had told her, laughing. "You produce wonderful babies, my pet, but enough is enough."

So there had been no more and thereafter her Christmas Days became a blur of happiness, the kinds of celebration varying only with the ages of the children, gifts changing from toys to adolescent treasures and at last to young adult possessions.

"I wish, Leonard darling, that you could have seen the first grandchild," she said now, her gaze fixed on the peak of the mountain, glowing in early sunset.

That would have been their happiest Christmas, the year Margaret's first child, Jimmy, was born, a little bundle of joy and mischief. Impossible to believe that now he was in college!

"You would have laughed all day, my darling, at his antics," she said aloud and laughed to herself at the very thought of what had never been.

When the children were almost grown came the years when Leonard took her with him on business trips. He was the head of his own company by then and they had traveled to Europe and sometimes even to Asia. It had seemed to her that everyone treated her as though she were a queen, and that was because he was the king. But they had always managed to be home for Christmas, what with the children growing up and getting married and she had talked of the grandchildren coming along, though Leonard had laughed at the idea of her being a grandmother.

"Didn't I tell you it was right for us to have the children when we were young? Now we can enjoy ourselves, doing whatever we like, for years to come."

Not so many years, at that, for nineteen years and thirteen days ago Leonard had come home at midday saying that he felt ill. His heart, so robust an organ all his life, had developed its own secret weakness, had suddenly stopped, beyond recall.

She stared out the window now, as the shadows of evening crept over the landscape. There was nothing more to say, for long ago all questions had been asked and answered, in some fashion or other. Only the eternal *why* remained and to that there was no answer. She sat in silence but strangely comforted. She had wanted to remember him clearly, and in remembering, he had come back to her.

At this moment she heard a knock on the door. With no sense of alarm she opened it and saw a man standing there, a man with a graying beard.

"I'm Andrew Bond, ma'am, a neighbor. My wife says she saw smoke here and I thought I'd better come over."

She put out her hand. "Why, Andrew Bond, your father used to look after the cabin for us. You've forgotten."

He stared at her. "No, I haven't forgotten—but are you here alone, ma'am?"

"Yes, for the day, that is. I came just to—well, I just came."

"Yes, ma'am. So you aren't staying?"

"No, if you'll dig me out tomorrow morning?"

"Yes, ma'am, I'll be glad to."

"Will you come in?"

"No, thanks. Wife's got supper on and she doesn't like to wait!"

"Well, thank you for coming, Andrew. And I hope you had a merry Christmas."

"Well, my wife and me, we've had a happy Christmas, anyway. Our son come home from Vietnam—wounded, but alive."

"I'm glad he's alive," she said fervently, as though he were someone she knew. But she was really glad.

"Thank you, ma'am," he said. "I'll see you in the morning, ma'am."

"I'll see you in the morning," she echoed.

She closed the door and lit the lamp and heaved another log on the fire. She decided she would eat something and then go to bed early. Tomorrow she would be home again, ready to see them all, the children and their children. She had had her day, her Christmas Day. She went to the window and stood looking out into the gathering darkness. . . . Happy? Who knows what that is?

No, wounded—but alive!